Frederick H. Christian

Sud … er

Ba … ted by

… NGE

CORGI BOOKS
TRANSWORLD PUBLISHERS LTD
A National General Company

To A
Second son,
second book.

SUDDEN—TROUBLESHOOTER

A CORGI BOOK 0 552 08907 9

First publication in Great Britain

PRINTING HISTORY

Corgi Edition published 1967
Corgi Edition reprinted 1968
Corgi Edition reprinted 1970
Corgi Edition reissued 1972

This book is set in Baskerville 10 pt.

Corgi Books are published by Transworld Publishers, Ltd.,
Cavendish House, 57–59 Uxbridge Road, Ealing,
London, W.5.

Made and Printed in Great Britain by
Richard Clay (The Chaucer Press) Ltd., Bungay, Suffolk.

Lafe Gunnison had passed the word to the homesteaders—quit stealing cattle or take the consequences! Up in the Mesquites, the nesters reacted the only way they knew: they told Gunnison he was a liar and if he showed up in their neck of the woods he'd wind up with a tombstone over his head.

It was trouble—big trouble—all it needed was one small spark to start a war to the death. Only one man could stop it. One man—backed by his courage and the guns he wore. A man with a past, scouring the West for two killers—a man called—Sudden.

Other Sudden Westerns by OLIVER STRANGE

SUDDEN—OUTLAWED
SUDDEN
THE MARSHAL OF LAWLESS
SUDDEN PLAYS A HAND
SUDDEN—GOLDSEEKER
SUDDEN MAKES WAR
SUDDEN RIDES AGAIN
SUDDEN TAKES THE TRAIL
THE RANGE ROBBERS
THE LAW O' THE LARIAT

By FREDERICK H. CHRISTIAN

SUDDEN STRIKES BACK
SUDDEN AT BAY
SUDDEN—APACHE FIGHTER
SUDDEN—DEAD OR ALIVE!

and published by CORGI BOOKS

CHAPTER ONE

'CAN yu use that gun, or is it jest to stop yu from blowin' away?' The words might have been, delivered in another tone of voice, nothing more than jest. In the present circumstances, however, no one could doubt that they were seriously intended. The scene was a typical Western saloon. A long bar, with shelves of shining bottles behind it, extended the length of the left-hand wall, and on the boarded, sanded space in front were tables and chairs for those who preferred to drink sitting down. The building was shaped like an 'L', and the shorter arm contained a cleared space for use as a dance hall. A staircase in the centre of the building led to an upper storey with a balcony running around the saloon; there, rooms were let to itinerants, and the girls who worked in the saloon lodged in the rest. Hanging kerosene lamps, surrounded by moths, provided light and there were mirrors, pictures of a crude kind, and animal heads mounted on the walls.

The man who had spoken stood in an aggressive stance by the bar. A thickset, beetle-browed individual of well over six feet, dressed in a coarse flannel shirt, homespun pants shoved into the tops of scuffed high boots, slouched hat, and heavy gunbelt, his harsh voice left no doubt that the words had no humorous intent.

'Dancy's in a bad mood tonight,' one of the onlookers murmured.

'Never knowed him have a good 'un,' returned the listener.

Dancy glowered at the object of his scorn, a youngster —he looked no more than nineteen—dressed in range garb that was notable only because its newness emphasised the wearer's unfamiliarity with it. The heavy gunbelt hung awkwardly on the boy's slim hips. Those watching, hardbitten veterans of frontier life, had a word for kids like this one: 'tenderfoot'. But if he was a tenderfoot, the boy was trying as hard as he could to conceal his dismay at being the centre of attention.

'You talkin' to me?' The lad strove manfully to keep his voice level, without complete success.

'Nope,' Dancy told him. 'I'm addressin' that jasper sitting on a camel behind yu.'

He roared with laughter at his feeble joke; one or two of his cronies sniggered and the boy flushed. The bartender moved cautiously along the bar, his hands well in view.

'C'mon Jim,' he expostulated. 'Let the kid alone. Have another drink!'

Dancy whirled, his face twisted angrily, and the bartender quailed. 'When I want yore rotgut I'll ask for it, Tyler!' roared the big man. 'If Lightnin' here was needin' yore aid, he'd be askin' for it—right, Lightnin'?' This to the youth, whose eyes were moving from face to face, as if in truth, pleading for help. No one in the room, however, seemed predisposed to step forward. Jim Dancy's liquor rages were well known to the inhabitants of Yavapai, and were treated like natural disasters. You stayed well out of harm's way while they were around, and afterwards repaired the damage as best you could, meanwhile thanking the Lord that it hadn't been any worse. Jim Dancy in a whisky haze was twice as dangerous as Jim Dancy sober, and Dancy sober was known to be a handy man with a six-shooter.

'I'm not . . . I ain't lookin' for trouble,' whispered the boy, backing as Dancy took two steps towards him.

'Well, ain't that amazin',' Dancy sneered. 'There yu was, not lookin' for trouble, an' trouble's gone an' come a lookin' for yu.' The whimsy left his voice and his eyes squinted piggily at the boy. 'I ast yu a question, Lightnin'. Is that shootin' arn an ornyment, or can yu use it?'

The boy, hypnotised by the big man, muttered, 'I . . . can . . . I can use it, if I have to. But . . .'

'Oho!' Dancy made an exaggerated leer of terror at this statement. 'So: a mouse with teeth!' He took two lurching steps backwards and surveyed the youth from head to foot, like a man appraising a horse he was contemplating buying.

'How long yu been in this territory, anyways?' he asked.

'On'y ... a couple o' weeks,' offered the youngster. 'I come from Philadelphia.' His chin lifted slightly. 'I'm plannin' on being a cowboy.'

'A *what*?' Dancy's scorn was elephantine. 'Yu—a puncher? If that ain't——'

The boy's face set, and he half turned as though to leave.

'—wait up, there, Lightnin'!' growled Dancy. 'I ain't through talkin'.'

'Well, I'm through listening,' the boy retorted defiantly. 'Just leave me alone.'

'An' if I don't...?' Dancy let the question hang in the air as he dropped all pretence of banter. The appearance of a cold killer dropped upon his shoulders like a mantle, and his hand clawed above the smooth butt of his Colt's ·45·

The boy regarded him with a mixture of dread and surprise; as though he could not comprehend his danger, and yet at the same time fully realised that he had no choice. He could either turn and run like a scared rabbit or face this bully on his own terms and probably be killed. His face set, and an unholy light kindled in Dancy's eyes.

'Damfool kid's too proud to run,' whispered one denizen of Tyler's with awe in his voice. 'Dancy'll kill him shore.'

Some customers, sensing the imminence of gunplay, shuffled hastily out of the possible line of fire. Nobody relished the duel; it was a cinch the kid was going to get killed. But nobody relished the idea of interfering with Jim Dancy in this mood, either.

The air grew tense. Dancy glared at the youngster and snapped, 'Make yore play, Lightnin': slap leather or eat crow!'

Without warning, a shot rang out, and a faint trickle of blood oozed from Dancy's left ear. The boy completely forgotten, he wheeled with a screech of pain to face the direction from which the shot had come, his hand flying almost automatically towards his holstered gun.

'That'd be a mistake.' A certain steeliness in the quiet voice stopped Dancy's hand as if it had been frozen solid. The speaker was a tall, lithe man in his late twenties, me give yu cause.' Picking up Dancy's shotglass of whisky from the bar, he tossed its contents full into the man's face. Spluttering and cursing, the big man pawed the fiery liquid from his eyes. Green followed him as he reeled backwards. His open hand slapped the man's face: right, left, and right again, bending Dancy backwards across the bar.

'Well...' he gritted. 'Where's that big tough feller I seen here a minnit ago?'

Dancy, his face purple with shame at being treated in this humiliating fashion before the whole town, sobbed in rage. Damn the man! His fingers itched to reach for his gun, longed to kill this ruthless intruder who had so disgraced him. But he could not do it.

'Like I thought,' said Green. 'Plain yeller, through an' through.'

He half turned away, as though in disgust, and in that split second Dancy acted. His hand clawed for his gun, the dark visage distorted with killing hatred. Even as he moved, Green whirled, and with every ounce of his wiry frame behind it, his clenched fist caught the would-be murderer flush on the point of his meaty jaw. The blow made a sound like an axe hitting a butcher's slab, and Dancy went backwards in a windmill of arms and legs, crashing into an upright and caroming off it to fall headlong against a wall. He slid down the wall to the floor senseless, and Green stepped across and relieved him of his gun. He presented it butt first to the bartender, who accepted it open-mouthed. A perfect hubbub of noise and conversation started up as every man in the bar discussed with his neighbour what had just been enacted before their eyes.

'Mr. Green,' said the bartender. 'I'm thankin' yu from the bottom o' my heart. Dancy would have killed this youngster shore as my name's Tom Tyler.'

The young man who had been the object of Dancy's initial attention pushed forward. 'I'd like to thank yu, too, Mr. Green,' he said. 'I'm proud to know any man who can throw a punch like that.'

Green turned to face the young man.

'What's yore name, kid?' he asked.

'Henry, sir. Henry Sloane.'

'Is that right, yu aim to be a cowboy?' The kid nodded. 'Ain't much of an ambition,' Green told him. 'Yu could just as easy get someone to kick yore brains out here in town. Quicker, too.'

Henry joined in the general laughter at Green's wry description of cowboy life.

'I came all the way from Philadelphia to find a job as a cowboy,' he told Tyler. 'My old man was a cowboy down Prescott way.' The old bartender nodded sagely, while Green listened with interest. 'I spent all my money buying this rig.' The kid turned to Green. 'Is it ... is something wrong with it, Mr. Green?'

Green smiled. 'Nothin' that two days in the saddle won't cure,' he told the youngster. 'An' listen: Jim's a sight easier than all this misterin' yo're doin'. Out here we don't reckon to call nobody mister less'n we' got to. Besides, yu make a man feel right ancient.'

The boy smiled. This drawling stranger who had saved his life was a totally different kind of man to the scowling bully who had been his first real contact with the West.

'Well, that's all about me,' he said. 'Now, where are yu from?'

Tyler shook his head and laughed when Green replied, 'I'm from over yonder, kid.' He tapped the youngster on the shoulder and told him, 'That's somethin' yu better learn not to ask in these parts, kid. It ain't considered perlite—or healthy—to ask a man where he's from or why he's travellin'.'

'Yu see,' enjoined a friendly onlooker, 'he might have trouble on his tail an' not want to talk about....' His voice tailed off as he realised that the stranger who had treated Dancy so cavalierly might well misconstrue what he had said, and take the words personally. But the tall cowboy smiled.

'No offence, old-timer,' he told the man. 'I ain't on the dodge.'

'Glad to hear that,' interposed a cold voice, and Green turned to face a slim, fair-haired man with keen eyes, and a wary smile. On his shirt pocket was pinned a five-pointed star which bore the legend 'Marshal'.

'I'm Appleby, town marshal,' he introduced himself. 'I

heard about the fracas. Yo're new in town, I take it. Passin' through?'

'Seein' the country,' Green told him disarmingly, 'but I had given some thought to lookin' for work in these parts. My belly's been thinkin' someone slit my throat.'

Appleby frowned.

'Yu've shore gone the wrong way about findin' work in these parts,' he told the cowboy. 'Jim Dancy happens to ramrod the Sabre ranch. I ain't shore he'd recommend yu to his boss after yu knocked his teeth out.'

The befuddled Dancy was struggling to his feet now, aided by the none-too-gentle hands of one or two of the saloon's regulars.

'Get yore damn' hands off me,' he snarled. 'I can manage.'

He stood, rocking slightly on his feet and glaring at Green as Appleby walked across to him.

'Yo're lucky yu ain't bein' patted in the face with a spade on Boot Hill,' the Marshal told him coldly. 'Get on yore horse an' get out o' town.'

For a moment Dancy's eyes locked with those of the fair-haired lawman, then they fell.

'Okay, Marshal, okay,' he mumbled. 'I'm goin'.' He shuffled out of the saloon, and Appleby turned back towards Green, who was talking to the bartender, Tyler.

'Yu say there's only a couple o' small spreads up in the hills?' he was asking the drink dispenser.

'Yep,' said that worthy. 'Up in the Mesquites, about three hours from town. Biggest is Jake Harris; the others are on the "one-o'-these-days" side.'

Green nodded. Smaller spreads were often so called because of the number of times their owners would tell anyone who cared to listen that 'one o' these days' he was going to be the biggest rancher in these parts.

'Yu know if they need men?'

'They'll be mighty pleased to see yu,' Tyler told him. 'They can on'y offer yu grub, a place to sleep, an' workin' pay, against Sabre's top wages, free cart'idges, good grub.'

'If that scum is a sample o' their crew I'd say Sabre'd pay to avoid,' Green remarked.

'They ain't over-popular,' Tyler told him, 'but . . .'

'Tyler, yo're just gossipin',' Appleby cut in. 'No use in

givin' anyone any wrong notions.'

'What do yu mean, seh?' asked the cowboy. Young Sloane pushed closer to hear.

'We got the makin's o' some trouble in these parts,' the Marshal told them. 'We've had smaller outfits movin' in over the last few years, an' homesteadin' in the Mesquites. A few of 'em ain't no better than they oughta be. Gunnison—he owns the Sabre—claims he's been losin' beef, an' that the homesteaders are responsible. He's added a few hard cases like Dancy to his payroll an' he keeps on threatenin' to ride up there one o' these days an' clear out Harris, who's the leadin' light o' the hill ranchers, an' all his friends.'

'What do Harris an' his people say about all this?'

'They claim Gunnison is just plain greedy, an' wants all the range for hisself. They call him a damn' liar an' swear they never touch any o' his beef. If they do, I ain't been able to find any sign of it.'

'But the Sabre is still losin' stock, huh?'

'Gunnison's got the figgers to prove it,' the Sheriff told him. 'It ain't really any o' my business: my job's to keep the town in order, but with the nearest law down in Tucson, somebody's got to poke around.'

'Sounds like a bad situation,' Green said reflectively.

'One o' these days the whole shebang is a-goin' to bile over,' Tyler said sombrely. 'When that day comes, I'd as lief be in Montana.'

'Well, I'm thankin' yu gents for tellin' us how the land lies. It don't look like we got much choice: I got a feelin' the Sabre wouldn't take to us any more'n their ramrod did.'

He turned to young Henry Sloane.

'What yu say, Philadelphia? Yu care to ride up to the Mesquites with me?'

The kid nodded, his eyes shining with something already close to devotion. 'Shore, Jim,' he said, trying to imitate Green's drawl.

'What's that man's name yu said: Harris?' asked Green.

'Jake Harris,' the bartender told him. 'Owns the JH spread. Yu tell him I sent yu.' He gave the cowboy directions to the Harris ranch. Green nodded his thanks and, with a smile and a nod to the Marshal, led the way out of Tyler's saloon, closely followed by the kid.

The saloon-keeper watched him go and then turned to the Marshal. 'Wal, Tom,' he said, 'I reckon that young feller could cool down this war talk in no time flat, an' I feel good for the first time in months. The drinks are on the house!' he shouted. Only the Marshal did not join in the general mêlée that ensued. He leaned against the bar, reflectively, eyeing the doorway through which the newcomer to Yavapai had left.

CHAPTER TWO

HENRY SLOANE thought of a hundred questions to ask the tall, saturnine man at his side as they rode out of town along the trail leading north towards the timbered hills they could see faintly in the distance, but he held his tongue and covertly surveyed his companion. Green's range garb was neat and serviceable, but hardly new. His saddle was plain and unadorned, but the leather had the deep dull glow that comes only from constant care. Green's horse, a magnificent black stallion, bore no brand except the letters 'JG' which had been hair-branded—plucked out with a knife blade rather than a hot iron—on the glossy haunches. Henry's eyes kept straying to the two tied-down guns at Green's sides, and eventually, his youthful curiosity unable to contain itself any longer, burst out, 'Jim, where d'yu ever learn to shoot like that?' To the kid's chagrin, Green's face darkened. His heart sank, and he wondered what he had said. After a moment, however, a smile reached Green's wintry countenance, and he replied, 'She's a long story, Philadelphia, but I'll tell yu this: yu don't learn in three days.'

'Gee, I know that, Jim. I just wondered.... I never even had a chance to thank yu properly until now.'

'Shucks,' Green told him. 'I had a reason for interferin'.'

'Yu did?' cried Henry, incredulously. 'What was it?'

'Wal,' grinned the cowpuncher, 'if Dancy had salivated yu, it would'a' given yu a mighty pore impression o' Arizona.'

His faint smile widened as the boy frowned, and then, as the import of what Green had said suddenly dawned on him, Henry burst out laughing.

'Yo're right,' he said, giggling. 'That ain't no way to see the country—from underneath!'

Green smiled to himself. Philadelphia was already getting the hang of the western way of looking at things.

'Three or four weeks an' he'll look like the genuine article,' Green mused. The kid broke in on his soliloquy with another question.

'Jim ... would yu learn me how that fast draw goes?'

'Philadelphia,' Green told him. 'The answer's no. The less yu know about gunfightin' the better off yu'll be.'

'Heck, Jim,' protested the lad. 'If I'm goin' to make a hand, I reckon I'll need to know how to shoot properly.'

'Shootin's one thing,' Green said, as they cantered over a bridge across a deep dry creek bed, the horses making a noise like thunder with their hoofs. 'Fast drawin's another. Any danged fool can do fast draws in front of a lookin' glass until he's convinced hisself he could outdraw his own reflection. But that ain't the same as facin' a man who's shootin' back.'

'But a fast draw is important, ain't it, Jim?'

'Shore 'nuff,' Green agreed. 'But what's more important is what yu do when yu've unlimbered yore smokepole. Hold up a minnit.'

He reined in his horse and, gesturing the lad to follow suit, tethered the animal to a mesquite bush beside the trail. He then paced off about fifteen yards and, stooping, piled up three or four large stones to make a pile. Upon this he placed a cardboard cartridge box which he had taken from his saddlebag. Walking back, he gestured with his chin at the makeshift target.

'There yu go, Philadelphia. Let's see what yu can do.'

Nothing loth, Henry settled himself, checked his gunbelt to see that the holster was hanging properly, drew clumsily, and fired. His shot whined off a rock somewhere in the distance.

'Never come near it,' smiled Green. 'Try her again.'

Sheathing the pistol, the youngster drew and fired again, and this time kept firing until the gun was empty. His shots kicked up dust not far from the pile of stones, while one nicked a branch which slewed down lop-sidedly from a tree, shedding leaves like snowflakes and sending a startled jay scolding away into the hills. Green tapped the downcast youngster on the shoulder.

'Philadelphia, yo're doin' her all wrong. Yore holster's too low, yo're too tight, yo're not aimin' ... now, watch.'

Without seeming to think about what he was doing, Green drew faster than Henry's eyes could see. Like a roll of thunder five shots blasted out in one staccato burst and the carton was torn off the pile of stones, whipped away to the right by the second shot, caught in flight by the third and the fourth, and whisked off in tatters by the fifth. Before Henry could bring his startled gaze back from where the box had landed to his companion, Green's gun was back in the holster.

'Holy cow, Jim,' breathed Henry. 'I never seen anything like it!'

Green's smile was wintry again. He looked older and tired, but he smiled as he saw the youngster's shining eyes.

'Philadelphia,' he said. 'There ain't no secret to it. Given good reflexes an' plenty o' practice, most fellers can learn to shoot pretty good. What counts is not so much knowin' how but knowin' *when* to use a gun.'

The youngster nodded. 'I get yu, Jim.'

'Yu listen to me, kid. Don't never pull a gun unless yu got to; and when yu got to, aim to shoot. Will yu remember that?'

'Shore, Jim,' the lad agreed. 'I swear it.'

'Good,' nodded Green. 'Now let's get that belt right for a start.' He adjusted the gunbelt around Philadelphia's middle until the butt of the pistol hung level with the lad's mid-forearm. He stood by the youngster's side and demonstrated the movements of the draw, chanting the sequence out aloud: 'Draw, cock, aim–fire!'

'Point the barrel like a finger,' he told Philadelphia. 'Yu ain't got time to sight. Imagine the gun-barrel is yore finger. Point it. Then fire.'

Together they went through the routine again. Draw, cock aim–fire; draw, cock, aim–fire. Draw, cock, aim–fire. Green's voice chanted on and on as Philadelphia's hand and arm grew heavier and heavier. His mentor finally called a halt.

'Gosh, Jim, my arm feels like it weighs about a ton,' he confessed.

'Yo're usin' new muscles,' Green told him. 'Don't worry: yu'll get used to it.'

He stood to one side, eyeing his young companion critically.

'Wal, yo're as ready as yu'll ever be. Try her yoreself.'

Henry nodded, his eyes gleaming at the prospect of testing his newly acquired knowledge. Already he had the feel of the gun, and the adjustments Green had made to the belt had made it feel as though it belonged about his waist. At a signal from Green he drew smoothly, the hammer clicking on the empty chamber.

'Pretty good, Philadelphia,' Green told him. 'Ain't much else I can teach yu; the rest is all practice.'

Henry nodded. He drew the gun again, and again. Pretty fast, he told himself.

'One final thing,' Green said. 'We'll draw together, see how much yu've learned.'

Henry nodded eagerly. 'I know I can't match yu, Jim,' he said. 'But I aim to try, so watch out.'

Green nodded, busy emptying his own revolver. Henry meanwhile settled himself in the half crouch that the puncher had shown him and, waiting until Green nodded, called, 'Draw!'

He had hardly touched the butt of his gun when he found himself staring into the muzzle of Green's forty-five.

'I ain't showin' off, Philadelphia,' the cowboy told him. 'I just want to impress on yu the final lesson I was talkin' about. If that had been for real, yu'd have been on yore way to Boot Hill right now. Remember: yu'll allus meet someone who's faster on the draw than yu are, so don't fool yoreself—not ever.'

He said this with such grim authority that Philadelphia's heart sank.

'Jim,' he asked hesitantly, 'did yu ever meet anyone faster'n yu?'

'I seen a few men I wouldn't have wanted to draw against, kid,' Green told him. 'Learnin' when to keep yore gun in the hotlster's durn near as important as knowin' when to pull her out. But that's enough, I reckon. We'd better be movin' on if we want to reach Harris's afore nightfall. An' keep that hawgleg unloaded while yo're practicin', yu hear me? I don't want yu shootin' yoreself in the laig.'

With a grimace, the youngster proceeded to his horse and mounted, following his friend back on to the trail. His mind was full of the fantastic display of shooting skill he had just witnessed, and he vowed silently to practice and practice until he could merit the unqualified praise of this tall, drawling cowpuncher who had in such a short time replaced any hero he had ever had.

* * *

The two riders traversed a wide, flat prairie, moving steadily uphill now towards the hills ahead of them. Off to the right a shimmer that looked almost like the sea drew their attention.

'Desert,' explained Green succinctly. 'Probably runs into badlands.'

The Mesquites were not much more than rolling foothills skirting the base of a range of mountains whose silvered tips they could see limned against the dropping sun. These were the Yavapais where, in not too distant time, the Apaches had lurked. From these mountains they had swept down upon the plains below, raiding south into Mexico, looting and killing, until the U.S. Army had subdued them and placed them on reservations where, even today, they lived in sullen acceptance of the white man's laws.

The two riders found themselves crossing a timberline, and riding into the gloom of a heavy pine forest. The keen scent of the green trees was strong in the evening air, the shade and coolness doubly welcome after the heat of the open plain. Ahead of them lay a junction; the trail dividing into four tracks.

'Second trail from the left, that bar-keep said,' Green

recalled. 'Better ride behind me, Philadelphia.'

Some minutes later they crested a bluff to see below them a small ranchhouse, constructed of logs, smoke curling lazily from its tin chimney. They could see men moving about in the open yard before the house. As they came fully into view it seemed to Philadelphia that the men moved more quickly, and one of them went into the house and emerged again. The gleam of the late sun on metal was discernible.

'Take off yore gunbelt an' sling it on the pommel o' yore saddle,' Green told his companion, suiting his own action to the words. Then, riding easily, his hands in plain sight, he kneed his horse on towards the ranch below. As they entered the ranch yard a thickset, bushy-browed individual stepped in front of them, covering them unwaveringly with a double-barrelled shotgun.

'Hold it right there,' he commanded. 'Johnstone—get their guns.'

A lanky fellow with fair hair that fell over his eyes and grew long at his collar stepped carefully forward and lifted the gunbelts off the pommels.

'Lookin' for Jacob Harris,' Green said cheerfully, as if no guns were in sight. 'Might yu be him?' he asked the thickset man.

'Might be,' allowed that individual. 'Depends who's askin'.'

'Name's Jim Green. Thisyere youngster is my partner. He goes by the name o' Philadelphia. Feller in town name o' Tyler said yu might have a job for two willin' workers.'

'Yu look a sight more like fodder for the Sabre, bucko,' growled Harris. 'Or maybe that's where yo're from?'

'It might be but it ain't,' smiled Green, slipping easily from the saddle, hands still held at chest height. 'But seein' yu got our guns, it ain't goin' to hurt yu none to listen.'

'I'm listenin',' Harris told him.

'Like I told yu, my name is Green. I'm a stranger in these parts. Been ridin' the chuckline atween here an' Tucson, an' I'm down to my last few dollars. It's either work or starve, so I'm hopin' for work, bein' what yu might call an optimist. The kid here is from Philadelphia, but his daddy was a cowman. He'll make a hand.'

The man named Johnstone sidled over to Harris and murmured something inaudible to the newcomers. Harris nodded.

'What Reb says is right, mister,' he told Green. 'Yu sport two guns, an' they look as if they've been used plenty. How come yu ride out here instead of tryin' Gunnison at the Sabre?'

'He gave Jim Dancy a beatin' in town, that's why!' burst out Philadelphia, unable to contain himself.

Harris looked at Green in astonishment.

'Yu did *what*?' He slapped his thigh. 'By cracky, mister, if yu did that yo're the most welcome sight I've seen in many a long day. Is what the kid says true?'

'Well, Dancy needed pacifyin' a mite,' Green admitted. 'He was set on marmalisin' Philadelphia, an' I kinda talked him out of it.'

'Yu shoulda seen him,' enthused Philadelphia. 'It was——'

'Shucks, kid, no call to run off at the mouth about it,' intervened Green. 'If it's okay with yu, seh, I'd be glad to lower my arms afore they stick like this.'

'Green, I'm beggin' yore pardon. Come on over here an' set.' Harris led the way to a bench on the porch of the ranchhouse. 'Yu, Reb, tell Susie to bring some cawfee out here for these fellers.' Johnstone rose and went into the house. 'Now, Mr. Green . . .' Harris began.

'. . . Jim's a sight easier, seh,' interposed the puncher.

'So be it, my boy, so be it. My name's Jacob, but purt' nearly everyone in these parts calls me Jake. Susie—that's my daughter; yu'll meet her just now—keeps on tellin' me I orta insist on Jacob like her Maw, God rest her soul, used to prefer. I keep on forgettin'. Now then, Jim: yu say yo're lookin' for work. Yo're a cattleman, I take it?'

'That's correct, seh,' Green told him. 'I hail from Texas.'

'An' the boy, here,' boomed Harris, 'is he . . .?'

'Nope, he's kinda apprenticed, yu might say,' the puncher replied. 'He'll work for his food an' a place to sleep an' mebbe a few dollars to spend in town, won't yu, Philadelphia?'

The younger man opened his mouth to frame an indignant protest at Green's apparent endorsement of legalised slavery, when at that moment they were interrupted by the arrival of Jake Harris's daughter, Susan. Not more than eighteen, her lithe young body had all the natural lissom grace of a young animal. Her neat shirt, jeans, and half-boots suited her admirably, while the late sun caught traces of gold in the cropped chestnut hair. Wide brown eyes, a slightly tip-tilted nose with a faint dusting of freckles, and a well-shaped mouth completed a picture that any man would have found attractive.

'Susie, thisyere is Jim Green. He's goin' to work for us. The young sprout, too. Goes by the name o' Philadelphia, believe it or not. My daughter, gents.'

'Gentlemen, I'm happy to know you.'

Susan Harris's voice was low pitched and warm. She smiled and set down steaming mugs of black coffee in front of them, affecting not to notice the hypnotised stare and open mouth of Green's companion. Philadelphia's reaction had not gone unnoticed by either Green nor his new employer. Jake Harris clapped the boy on the shoulder and shattered his reverie with jovial words.

'Son, yu ain't the first cowpoke to gawp at my gal, an' I don't reckon yu'll be the last, neither! Danged if she don't get purtier every day!'

'She shore don't hurt the eyes none,' Green agreed. Then to Philadelphia, 'Yu was about to say something afore Miss Susan arrove,' he prompted.

The boy gulped, flushing scarlet as he realised how completely he had betrayed himself. Green's smile told him the puncher was well aware that he had been about to protest his 'apprenticeship' when Susan Harris appeared, but seeking to spare his young friend's feelings further, Green asked a question of Harris.

'I run a small spread, Jim,' the old man said. 'Nothing to rave about, but she's more'n I can handle alone. About seven hundred head. Up to now I ain't been able to get help. My neighbours pitch in at round-up time, but they got their own places to look after.'

'That bartender Tyler said yu was on the "one-o'-these-days" side,' blurted Philadelphia.

'Damned if he ain't right,' chuckled Harris. 'I'm allus sayin' to Susie that one o' these days we'll spread a mite, an' build up our herd. But we'll never do it without help. I can't avoid feelin' that yu boys would'a' got a better deal at the Sabre. Gunnison pays top rates: I can't match that.'

'Who is this Gunnison, anyway?' asked Philadelphia. 'All I heard when I was in town was Gunnison said this, Gunnison did that, Gunnison wants the other. I got the feelin' he owned that town.'

'Durned if that ain't half true, boy,' Harris admitted. 'Lafe Gunnison is an old tyrant. Been here since the days when Pete Kitchen was fightin' Cochise's bucks, an' he reckons Gawd gave him a special lien on the Yavapai valley. I understand his feelin's. He come out here when things was a danged sight harder than they are now, an' fought Apaches for his land. He paid for it in blood an' sweat, but he never took the trouble to file on it legal an' proper until after we moved in here. Then it was too late to move us off. We're entitled to this land an' we're stayin' till hell freezes over.'

'Y'all said a mouthful, Jake,' said Johnstone, who had come up while the older man was talking. From his accent Green placed the man as a Southerner. 'We own this land legal, but Gunnison don't aim to let that stand in his way. He's told us in so many words: get out or take the consequences.'

'Yu had any trouble with him?'

'Not directly,' Harris told him. 'A few nuisance raids. Wheatfields flattened, steers stampeded, a couple o' horses stolen. Nothin' big. We complained to the Marshal, o' course, an' although it ain't his responsibility he went to see Gunnison. The old rascal claimed he knowed nothin' about it.'

'How many men on the Sabre?' Green wanted to know.

'About twenty-five, all told. Gunnison, his son Randy—a misfit if ever one was born—a cook, an' his riders. Last year or so he's taken on' a couple o' jaspers who know more about guns than cows or I miss my guess. I reckon that's some o' Randy's doin'.'

'How far apart are yore people up here?' was Green's next query.

'Not far, Jim, not far. Reb, here, is our nearest neighbour. His brand is the Star an' Bar'—he chuckled—'Reb's from Virginia.'

'I didn't reckon that was an Irish accent,' grinned the cowboy.

'It ain't that, for shore,' replied Johnstone.

'Reb's about five miles east o' here,' continued Harris. 'His land is next to Stan Newley's Circle Diamond. South o' them lies Terry Kitson's Running K spread. The other one is Taylor's Lazy T. He's to the northwest, about six miles, not far from the river. Yu saw that, o' course.'

'That's the one that runs east o' town a mite. We crossed a small creek, too, on the way up here.'

'That's Borracho Creek. Mex for "drunkard".'

Green and Philadelphia looked their interest, and Harris explained, 'The way she is right now, yu'd put her down as a little trickle, one o' them "two yards wide an' two inch deep" cricks. But yu noticed the crick bed?'

Green nodded. 'She's a flash stream?'

'Yo're right, my boy. One rainstorm up in the mountains an' that little crick turns into a ragin' monster that'll take a full-grown tree, root 'er up, an' toss her fifty yards in five seconds, an' kill a grown man in half that time. Yu, boy——!' He pointed at Philadelphia. 'You stay away from that crick, yu hear me? If it looks like rain in the hills, yu get a good fifty yards from there afore yu stop runnin'.'

'I'll remember, sir,' Philadelphia promised him.

'An' dang me if I aim to keep on callin' yu that stonebreaker of a name. Yu mind if I shorten yore monicker to Philly?'

The boy shook his head, smiling. At this moment Susan Harris came out of the house to collect their coffee mugs and to tell them that supper was ready.

'Yu boys'll want to wash up afore supper,' said Harris, rising. 'We can talk some more afterwards. I'll show yu where yu can leave yore gear. Tomorrow we can take a look at the country, an' I'll introduce yu to the rest of our people up here.'

Green stood, and his youthful partner followed suit.

His eyes kept straying constantly to the doorway through which Susan Harris had disappeared, although he tried hard to conceal his interest from those near by.

'Smack atween the eyes,' Green told himself. 'Pore old Philadelphia. Life won't be no bed o' roses for yu, my young friend. I got a hunch that there's a li'l lady who'll let yu chase her plenty afore yo're caught.'

The look in the kid's eyes told him, however, that it was a chase he would gladly join.

CHAPTER THREE

THE next day Jake Harris saddled up a horse, and the three men rode across his land to Newley's Circle Diamond, stopping only to wave down at Reb Johnstone, who was working in the corral outside his compact, if somewhat rickety, old frame house. Newley turned out to be a small, nervous, dark-haired man of perhaps fifty with a tendency to start sentences which he never finished. He stammered a welcome to them, and they stayed long enough to drink coffee with Newley before moving on southward to Kitson's Running K. Kitson turned out to be a heavily built man with a thatch of silvering hair. His smile was broad and friendly, and he was delighted to hear of Green's encounter with Dancy.

'Been waitin' for the day someone would trim that jasper's hair,' he chortled. 'Would'a' done it myself afore now, but Jake keeps tellin' us to stay outa trouble with the Sabre.'

'Yu got a nice place here,' remarked Green. 'Yu runnin' many head?'

'I don't run cattle,' Kitson told him. 'My speciality is horses. I got about sixty head. Sell 'em to the Army.'

'Good business,' commented Green. 'D'yu lose many?'

'Allus did lose one or two to the odd war party or long rider lookin' for a change o' hoss,' Kitson told them. 'Lately it's got so I lose a couple of head at a time. Never enough to get me real mad; just enough to make me wish Lafe Gunnison would fall down a hole an' break his stubborn ol' neck.'

'Yu ever see anyone actually liftin' yore stock?' was Green's question.

'No,' interposed Harris, 'they're too clever for that. We never do more than find the odd track here an' there. We've tried trailin' them, an' allus lose 'em up in the Mesquites. The pine needles are so thick up there a 'pache couldn't trail an elephant.'

'Yu run this place alone, Mr. Kitson?' asked Philadelphia.

'Not exactly, son,' was the reply. 'I got a hired hand, a big dumb Swede who don't understand a word I say. We share the work. He leaves it an' I do it.'

They rode off, after inviting Kitson over to the Harris house for supper that evening. They had already told Reb Johnstone to bring Stan Newley over. These two, who ran the smallest spreads and were, in fact, more like farmers than ranchers, concentrating upon wheat and barley crops rather than livestock, shared the work on their two places and had no hired hands.

They reached Taylor's spread at noon, and shared the rough lunch that Taylor and his two men were preparing when they arrived. Taylor was a short, compactly built man with a noticeable Scots burr in his voice. His riders were Jack Scott and Fred Peters; both men were tall, burned to the colour of leather on their hands and faces by years in the saddle.

'Jack used to be on the Sabre, years ago,' Taylor told his visitors. 'He quit when Randy Gunnison came back from Santa Fé.'

'Yu bet,' said the slow-talking Scott. 'That hombre'd make a saint cuss.'

'An' yu ain't no saint,' grinned Peters. 'Yo're right, though. Randy Gunnison gets my prize for the least-necessary man I ever met.'

'He sure ain't got many friends,' observed Green. 'I ain't heard a good word said about him since I come to this neck o' the woods.'

'Unlikely ye will, either, laddie,' Taylor told him. 'The boy is a complete wastrel, an' the despair o' his fayther's life. Old Lafe Gunnison has washed his hands o' the boy.'

'He seems to spend most of his time gallivantin' off to Phoenix or Tucson,' Jake Harris added. 'Or swillin' rotgut with some floozy in town.'

'Strange, that,' murmured Green. 'From what I've heard about old man Gunnison, he don't sound like a man who'd put up with that sort of shenanigans.'

'I reckon he's just given up on Randy, like everyone else in Yavapai,' Scott put in. 'His paw gives him no money, so he's allus in debt. What money he wins gamblin' he blows on women or booze.'

'Well, yu gentlemen o' leisure mayn't have much to do but I have,' Alexander Taylor told them, 'so oblige me by washin' yore crocks an' dryin' 'em afore ye leave.' He stamped out of the house, and in a few moments they heard the steady chock-chock of his axe biting into the tree he was felling. Scott and Peters winked at their guests, and followed the old man out after washing their plates and cups.

'He don't stand much on ceremony, does he?' gasped Philadelphia.

'Ah, take no notice, lad,' Harris laughed. 'That's Alex's way of avoiding hearin' yu thank him. He can't stand anyone thankin' him: just a quirk, I guess.'

They washed their dishes and trooped out of the house, mounting and riding across the yard towards where the three men were working. 'Watch this,' chuckled Jake Harris, and rode over to Taylor's side. 'We'll look for yu about eight, Alex,' he said. The Scot nodded, without looking up from his work. 'And Alex——' Taylor looked up enquiringly. 'Thanks very, very much indeed for the lovely meal ... hey!'

The last expletive was occasioned when the Scot, with a broad grin, suddenly threw his hands up under Harris's horse's nose. The animal, startled, tried to rear and turn in the same moment, and Jake had his work cut out to remain in the saddle. Taylor grinned at the watching visitors.

'I'll bet he told ye I didn't like bein' thanked,' he grinned. 'Now ye know he was right. Goodbye.'

And without a word he returned to his axe-work, while Peters and Scott pounded each other on the back at the sight of Jake Harris struggling to get his mount under control.

'Hey, Jake!' called Fred Peters. 'Don't mention it!'

'Bah!' snapped Harris, and wheeled his horse out of the yard and across country towards home, followed by his two new employees, broad smiles creasing their faces.

* * *

Later that evening all of the men that the newcomers had met that day were enjoying coffee in Harris's sprawling living-room. A big hanging lamp cast a warm light, and a fire crackled in the stone hearth, for the nights were cooler up in these hills. The room was a pleasant one; on the scrubbed floor several catamount pelts were scattered, and Susan Harris's touch was evident in the neat fringed cushions and the frilled curtains and the shining brass vases full of mountain flowers on the mantel above the fireplace.

'Boy, this is the life,' enthused Fred Peters. 'Any time yu want to come over to the Lazy T an' clean 'er up some, yu say the word, Miss Sue.'

'If yu wasn't so dadblasted lazy yu wouldn't need to ask,' put in his taciturn fellow rider.

'If I worked any harder they'd be nothin' for yu to do,' retorted Peters. 'I never did figger what yu do all day.'

'Mostly what yu oughta be doin' stead o' jawin',' Jack Scott told him.

'Listen to him,' grinned Peters. 'That's why Gunnison tossed him off the Sabre—couldn't get him to work any way at all.'

'This Gunnison hombre,' Green ruminated. 'I can't figger why he's so set on havin' yore land. After all, he don't need it. Jake was tellin' me Gunnison owns all the land west o' the river.'

'Just greedy, mebbe,' offered Kitson. 'Some men ain't happy if they don't own ever'thing in sight.'

'Plain stubborn, more likely,' Newley said hesitantly. 'He's allus been...' His voice tailed off.

'Dang me, Stan, if I ever hear yu finish a sentence I'm likely to pass out,' laughed Harris. 'Still, yo're probably more'n half right. Gunnison's been in this country so long he thinks he's some kind o' tin Gawd.'

'I see Jim's point, though,' Taylor said. 'When ye think about it, there has to be some reason for Gunnison wanting our land. I can't just put my finger on it, but it has to be something. He surely don't need the grass.'

'Tell me when all this trouble started,' Green suggested.

'About a year, eighteen months ago, more or less,' Harris told him. 'Gunnison roared an' made a lot o' noise when we first filed on this land, but we had no trouble.'

'Then these nuisance raids started?' prompted Green.

'That's right,' Kitson told him. 'Jake had a couple of men working here, but they soon quit. Couple of Sabre riders roughed them up about a mile from the house. They never would tell us who, but it had to be Sabre.'

'We figgered it was probably Dancy, but couldn't prove anything,' added Harris.

'They rode all over my wheatfield one night,' added Newley.

'Flattened a whole year's crop an' I couldn't...'

'Do a thang to stop them,' finished Reb Johnstone. 'Stan heah got a shot th'owed at him ev'ah time he poked his haid outa the do'r.'

'Tom Appleby, he'd ride up here, shake his head. Couldn't find no trace o' who done it,' Kitson said. 'I lost some horses. We trailed 'em to the edge o' the desert, but it was like tryin' to trail flyin' fish in the water.'

'Any gold or silver in these parts?' was Green's next query.

'Nary a trace, laddie,' Taylor told him. 'We get the odd desert rat pokin' around in the Yavapais, but nobody's ever found enough to buy bacon. Yo're away off course if yo're thinkin' we're sittin' on a gol' mine.'

Green shrugged. 'On the face of it, it looks like yo're right, then. Gunnison is just plain greedy.'

The talk turned to other things, and Susan Harris replenished their coffee cups. As she went around the room, Green covertly surveyed the assembled men. The meeting was a friendly affair, and it was plain to see that all these men were good friends, a close-knit group of individuals who accepted each other's weaknesses and strengths. 'Not a bad apple in the whole barrel,' Green thought as he watched them joshing Philadelphia, to whom for some reason Jake Harris had taken an inordinate liking. It was easy to see how they remained so determined in the face of Gunnison's hostility.

The sound of a horse's hoofs pounding up the trail put an instant stop to the conversation. Like well-drilled troops, Harris and his friends moved quickly around the room. Sue dimmed the big light, and Kitson moved a tall cast-iron screen in front of the fireplace, concealing the flicker of the flames. All of the men moved near windows, their ever-ready guns in their hands. The organisation impressed Green and he said as much in an undertone to Harris.

'We worked this drill out about two months ago,' Harris told him. 'Do her automatically now. If Gunnison decided to catch us all in one place we'd be sittin' ducks. Figgered it might be wise to surprise him if he tried it. We're nigh on eager to try her out.'

'Let's hope yu don't have to,' Green said. A quick glance about the room showed him Philadelphia standing guard over the crouched form of Susan Harris, who had knelt down behind the big sofa. Despite the tenseness of the moment Green smiled to himself.

A hail from outside brought a noticeable relaxation of the tension. 'That's Tom Appleby, ain't it?' said Peters.

'Sounds like him,' agreed Harris. He stepped near the door and shouted, 'That yu, Appleby?'

'Hello, Jake. Shore it's me. Open up!'

'Put up the lights,' Harris ordered, swinging the bar back from the door and opening it. 'Come on in, Tom.'

The slim figure of the town Marshal entered after a moment on the doorstep spent beating the dust from his clothes. For the first time Green noted the fact that the Marshal wore a tied-down holster on his left hip. 'Southpaw,' Green told himself, 'an' no slouch, either, by the look o' him.'

'Gents, good evenin',' Appleby nodded. 'Sorry to barge in.'

'What brings yu this far north, Tom?' asked Kitson.

'Just doin' my rounds, Terry,' was the cool reply. 'I wanted to check whether our friends found yu all right.'

'Yu mean, to see whether we're workin' here or on the

Sabre!' blurted Philadelphia. The Marshal favoured him with a sour look.

'I knowed yu didn't go to the Sabre,' he said. 'I just come from there.'

'How's Dancy?' asked Jack Scott. 'Sicker'n hell, I hope.'

'He'll survive,' Appleby told him. 'He won't look so purty without his front teeth, is all.'

Fred Peters chortled with delight, and danced over to pump Green's hand. 'Jim, yu shore done us a good turn comin' to Yavapai. That rooster's been needin' his comb trimmed for a while, now.'

Green smiled. 'I would've thought that was more in the Marshal's line. Ain't yu ever had occasion to pacify Dancy, Marshal?'

Appleby looked at Green sharply, but the puncher was smiling disarmingly. The Marshal shrugged.

'Green, yo're a stranger in these parts, so forgive me if I sound a mite on the pompous side. Normally, Dancy just gets loud; then he goes away someplace an' sleeps it off. Now an' then he gets in a brawl. Someone loses a few teeth or gets an arm broke—never anythin' that Dancy can't walk away from.'

'He was shapin' to drill me!' cut in Philadelphia.

'Wal, maybe, maybe not,' Appleby said. 'Be that as it may, Dancy's the foreman o' the Sabre, an' I have to bear that in mind when I tangle with him. It ain't——' He held up a hand to stop the remark that Green was about to make. 'It ain't a question o' playin' favourites. It's plain fact: if I ride the Sabre too hard, an' Gunnison decided to take his trade to Riverton, about fifteen miles upriver, Yavapai'd dry up an' blow away. Jake here'll tell yu I try to give everyone a fair shake. My job is to keep the peace in Yavapai. Outside town all I can do is try to help as much as possible.'

'It's true enough, Jim,' Reb Johnstone said. 'Tom heah does the best he can, all things considered.'

Appleby's smile was open and friendly, and it grew even wider as Susan Harris came into the room with the cup of coffee she had gone to make when the visitor's identity was established.

'Wal, now, I reckon this was worth the ride—a cup o' cawfee from the purtiest gal this side o' Tucson,' grinned the Marshal. 'How are you, Miss Susan?'

Sue Harris blushed and smiled. 'Well, thank you, Tom. We haven't seen you for a while.'

Green risked a sly glance at Philadelphia. The youngster was glowering at the Marshal, and the puncher smiled to himself.

'Got to admit it,' Appleby was saying. 'Been powerful busy tryin' to get a line on this lost Sabre stock.'

'Gunnison's lost more beef?' A worried frown appeared on Jacob Harris's face.

'A few head here, a few there. Nothin' big,' Appleby told them. 'Just enough to be noticed. Any o' yu boys seen any loose stock up in the hills?'

No one spoke; Scott and Peters shook their heads.

'Didn't expect yu would've,' Appleby said. 'Beats me. Yu can't even find tracks. It's as if someone was flyin' off with them.'

'Mighty peculiar. Yu ain't thinkin' ...?' said Kitson.

'Hell, no, Terry. Yu boys give me yore word yu wasn't lifting Sabre beef an' I believe yu. But Gunnison's losin' 'em just the same, an' yu can't blame him for feelin' hot about it. He swears it has to be yu boys. I keep tellin' him it ain't. It's deadlock.'

'Ol' goat,' muttered Jack Scott. 'He's slapped his brand on enough mavericks in his time.'

'I'm just tellin' yu what he said,' Appleby remarked. 'Ain't sayin' I agree. I'm just hopin' I can find suthin' out afore Lafe takes it into his head to go on the warpath.'

'He better come dressed fo' a buryin',' Johnstone snapped. 'He'll sho' be participatin' in one if he comes up heah with a war party.'

'Let's hope it don't come to that,' said Appleby. 'I wouldn't take much pleasure in standin' in the middle tryin' to keep yu boys an' the Sabre crew apart. In the meantime, if anybody has to go to town, mebbe it wouldn't be a bad idea to leave yore guns at home.'

'Fat chance o' that,' snorted Johnstone. 'No damyankees are goin' to scare me into shuckin' mah shootin' arn.'

'Just friendly advice, Reb.' The Marshal rose and picked up his wide-brimmed black hat. 'Miss Susan, thank yu for the cawfee. I'm lookin' forward to seein' yu in town right soon. Maybe I can return the compliment: Mrs. Robinson's restaurant serves a fair cup o' cawfee these days.'

'Yu'll have to stand in line, Tom,' laughed Fred Peters. 'There's about seventeen guys just waitin' for the chance.'

Appleby smiled. 'Shore,' he agreed, 'but how many o' them live in Yavapai?'

Bidding all those present goodnight, he went out, and they watched him mount and ride up the trail into the timber.

'Well, Jim,' asked Taylor when Appleby was out of sight. 'What d'ye think of our Marshal?'

'Pretty cool customer,' commented Green.

'I don't like the look o' him,' added Philadelphia.

'Hell, Philly, yo're a mite biased,' grinned Jack Scott, and Jake Harris roared with laughter as the boy flushed.

'Cool is about the right word,' Terry Kitson said to Green. 'He's pretty fast with that gun when he has to be. He runs a clean town an' he's tough. Even if he has to bend over backwards to stay in the middle o' the road.'

'Sounds durned uncomfortable to me,' was Philadelphia's comment, to which Jake roared out, 'Jumpin' jehosophat, Philly, don't yu fret none. Susie don't go to town *that* often!'

'Oh, Father!' snapped Susan, 'stop talking about me as if I weren't in the room. Tom Appleby is a gentleman, and don't you forget it.'

'I won't,' chortled her parent, unabashed. 'Don't yu forget, neither: a gentleman is only fifty per cent gentle; all the rest is man.'

To which remark Susan, having no adequate reply, tossed her head and flounced out of the room.

CHAPTER FOUR

Susan Harris pulled her horse to a stop, and Philadelphia reined in his own animal, dismounting to tether the two beasts to a nearby tree. Sue's face was flushed and shining from the gallop, and her dark hair was disarrayed prettily. The little glade in which they had stopped offered a welcome oasis of shade on the open prairie, and a small brook babbled cheerfully on its way down to the Yavapai river.

'Oh, I did enjoy that,' she told Philadelphia, 'didn't you, Philly?'

'Shore, did, ma'am,' was his enthusiastic reply. 'This is a mighty purty country.'

She looked at her companion quizzically. 'You sound more like Jim Green every day, do you know that?'

The youngster flushed. 'He's a fine man, Miss Susan.'

'He must have impressed you greatly to inspire such devotion.'

'He saved my life,' Philadelphia told her simply.

'Yes, I know,' replied the girl thoughtfully. 'I still cannot imagine why that awful man Dancy picked on you.'

'Just lucky, I guess,' said the boy, whimsically. 'It wouldn't be so one-sided if he tried it now.'

'Oh, Philly, really. You mustn't think that practicing with that silly gun is going to keep you out of trouble. In the end guns only make things worse.'

'That ain't true, Miss Susan,' he said. 'There's some men yu can only convince that way.'

'Philly,' she said, appalled at this statement, 'yu can't really believe that!'

'Can, an' do,' the youngster assured her. 'An' I aim to keep on practicin' in case I meet any o' them.'

She looked at his set face and knew that he was not joking. 'No one would ever believe that you have only been out West a few weeks, Philly. You already sound like a Westerner.' She smiled. 'You even look the part.'

The compliment pleased the young man mightily. In truth, the days spent in the open, the hard work, and the simple fare had greatly changed the pasty-faced youngster who had been bullied in Tyler's by the Sabre foreman. The clothes, once raw and new, were already faded by the bleaching Arizona sun, and the pallor of the city streets had been replaced by a healthy tan. Philadelphia's whole bearing was different, and his hitherto slight frame had filled out.

The girl asked another question.

'Why did you come to Arizona, Philly?'

'I guess I allus wanted to,' he told her. 'My ol' man was a cowboy, down Prescott way.'

'Really? You never told me that.'

'Never talked about it much. Yu see, I never knew him.'

'Oh, I'm sorry,' the girl said contritely, 'I shouldn't pry.'

'He—heck, ma'am, that's all right,' he reassured her. 'My mother was born in Philadelphia, yu see, an' she ran away from home to marry my Pa. They met when she was visiting some folks in Phoenix. He was just an ordinary cowpuncher, thinkin' o' startin' up on his own. When they got married her family disowned her.'

The girl made no reply, but her downcast eyes encouraged him to continue.

'She must have had a tough life,' Philadelphia continued. 'It was pretty hard in them days. When I was born she was so ill that my Pa sent her back to her family, an' she took me with her, leaving my brother an' my Pa in Prescott.'

'And she never went back?' Susan asked, aghast.

'I don't know exac'ly what happened,' the young man confessed. 'She never would talk much about it. I allus figgered the family just wouldn't let her go back, an' my Pa never come to fetch her. All I recall about him was that he was a tall man with long black hair, an' big gentle hands. I suppose he's dead.'

'Didn't you try to find him when you came to Arizona?'

'Shore I tried,' Henry exclaimed, 'but I didn't have much to go on. My mother would never talk about my Pa, an' I had no one else to ask. All I knew was that he called the ranch the Lazy L. When Mother died, I found some letters, but they was just signed "yore lovin' husband", which warn't much help. Nobody down in that part o' the country remembered any Lazy L ranch run by a big black-haired man with a son about ten. It was hopeless. Like I said, I reckon he's dead.'

'Oh, Philly,' she said, 'I'm sorry. I didn't mean to pry...'

'Shucks, that's all right, Miss Susan. I wanted yu to know, anyways,' he told her. He said no more, but Susan, wise beyond her years, knew that there was much left unsaid. They were silent for a long moment, and then she rose, her manner thoughtful.

'I can understand how your mother must have felt,' she told him as they untethered the horses. 'Often, I think about what will happen to me...'

'Gosh, ma'am, I thought yu loved it here!' blurted Philadelphia.

'I do,' she told him. 'I love the country, and the people. But marriage...' Her voice tailed away, and then her chin lifted. 'I'm going to look after Daddy,' she said. 'No quarter section as a cowboy's wife for me. I want to see the world, have fine clothes, and a lovely home. I don't want to turn into an old woman before my time, looking after a house full of children.'

Having thus crushed the seeds of every dream, hope, and ambition in her escort's mind, the lovely Susan Harris mounted her horse and turned him towards home. She was leading the way out of the little glade at a canter when a shot rang out and her horse fell, screaming, throwing her heavily from the saddle.

Philadelphia reined his horse in sharply, so sharply that the shot which followed, and which might have blasted him out of his saddle, buzzed by his head like an angry hornet. His gun already in his hand, the youngster charged full tilt at the hillock about fifty yards distant from behind which he had caught a flash of light. Without thought he emptied his gun in the direction of the would-be assassin as he careered towards the ambuscade. Another shot rang out and Philadelphia cartwheeled backwards out of his saddle to the ground, a thin trickle of blood oozing from his scalp. He lay there, half unconscious, as the muffled thunder of hoofs receded and the unseen assailant made good his escape. Then a quick, dark cloud descended over his mind, and he plummeted into a dark, never-ending abyss.

* * *

James Green had been checking the herd with Jake Harris when faintly in the distance they heard the shots, the flatter crack of the rifle followed by the popping of Philadelphia's six-shooter, then the final flat sound of the rifle again. The two men looked at each other grimly.

'Sounds like it came from over that way,' Green offered, nodding towards the low hills to the South. Harris nodded. 'Probably down by—my God! Philly an' Sue rode down that way! Come on!'

He dug in his spurs and rocketed away, Green thundering in his wake. Together they swept across the open plain for two or three miles until a fringe of trees broke the horizon. 'Glade ... Susie often goes there ...' Green heard Harris shout as they thundered along. Within a few more minutes they were on the scene of the ambush, and Harris gave a mighty cry of relief as he saw his daughter sitting upright on the ground, shaking her head. Green espied his young friend lying off to the right and swung Nigger around. Dismounting, and turning the boy over, he breathed a sigh of thanks as he saw that the trickle of blood across the boy's brow stemmed from a raw gash across the side of his head.

'Creased,' he muttered. 'But who ...?'

His brown furrowed, he lifted down his canteen from the saddle and was forcing some water between the youngster's lips as Jake Harris came over with the still-dazed Susan.

'Some jasper threw shots at the pair of 'em,' Harris growled. 'Dropped Susie's hoss an' then it looks like he tried to kill the kid.'

Philadelphia's eyes fluttered, and he suddenly sat up. 'Sue!' he cried, trying to struggle to his feet.

'It's all right, son,' Harris reassured him. 'Take it easy. She's fine.'

The boy relaxed as Green poured water on to his bandanna, wincing as the puncher cleaned the gash on his head. In a few terse words he described what had happened, while Harris and Green looked grimly at each other.

'They're stoopin' pretty low, shootin' at girls an' kids, now,' rumbled the old man.

'Daddy, Philly's not a kid,' said Susan with passion in her voice. 'If it hadn't been for him . . .' She stopped, and for no apparent reason blushed.

For the first time a trace of a smile touched Green's lips, but vanished immediately as he stood up and said, 'Let's take a look-see if Mr. Bushwhacker left any sign.'

Striding across to the hillock that Philadelphia had indicated, Green scanned the area with keen eyes. From this vantage point the trail leading out of the glade was easily covered, and he nodded to himself.

'Mr. Bushwhacker knowed his spot,' he murmured.' He musta hunkered down here someplace.' Casting around for a few more moments, he found a place where the earth was scuffed and the indentation of two boot-heels was clear in the earth. Back-tracking, mentally putting himself in the ambusher's place, it did not take Green long to discover where the would-be killer had hidden his horse. The lower foliage of a tree had been nibbled, and several branches bore evidence of chafing. The hoofprints showed that the animal had been restive. He was kneeling, studying these marks, when Harris, his daughter, and the now fully recovered Philadelphia came up.

'Nothin' much to go on,' he announced. 'Our bushwhackin' friend was mighty careful to pick up his shells, an' almost anyone coulda left those heel-marks.'

'Hell, Jim, who else could it 'a' been except one o' Gunnison's hirelin's?' demanded Harris, 'Who else'd want to take a shot at my gal?'

'Yu so shore it was Miss Susan they was really after?' queried the puncher.

'Why, Jim,' said Philadelphia, surprise in his voice, 'I don't know anyone in these parts! Why'd anyone want to take a shot at me?'

'Philadelphia, I figger yu rattled Mr. Bushwhacker chargin' at him like that. Mebbe all he aimed to do was throw a scare into Miss Susan. Likely she'd tell her daddy an' he'd get the message.'

'Yu think mebbe this was a warnin', Jim?' asked the

old man. 'To keep me mindful o' the fact that I could be hurt other ways than...'

'I ain't sayin' that's it,' Green said. 'It just might be, that's all.'

He hunkered down again and studied the tracks. Then he announced his decision.

'I'm goin' to follow his tracks,' he said. 'Jake, yu take Philly an' Miss Susan back to the JH.'

Harris nodded, his face sombre. 'Susie, yu can ride double with me. Let's go, Philly.'

'Not me,' declared that young worthy stoutly. 'I'm goin' with Jim.' His friend turned to remonstrate, but the boy said, 'Don't yu argue none with me—I'm the one got shot at, remember. I reckon I got a right.'

Green smiled. 'Mebbe yu do, at that. Okay, Jake, the kid stays. Yu ride on back. We'll see where Mr. Bushwhacker leads us.'

When they had gone, Green rolled and lit a cigarette. He sat down on a small rock and smoked in silence, the furrows deep between his brows.

'Harris is hard hit,' said his companion. Green nodded. Silence again ensued, and presently Philadelphia tried again:

'I reckon he hadn't thought they'd try to get at him through Miss Susan.'

'Mmm,' said Green, still busy with his thoughts.

'Dang me if yu ain't the tightest man I ever met with a word,' exploded Philadelphia. 'What does a feller have to do around here to get some reaction out o' yu—get shot through the head?'

His mentor looked up, and for the first time a wide grin crossed his face. 'Yu oughta thank yore lucky stars yu got a crease in yore scalp,' he told Philadelphia.

'How come?' that worthy wanted to know.

'Shucks, that's easy to answer,' was the reply. 'If yu'd been hit anyplace else it mighta done some damage. I reckon our bushwhacker didn't know he was aimin' at yore thickest part.'

Before his young friend could suitably reply to this insult the tall puncher was on his feet and striding across the clearing to where Nigger stood patiently cropping the grass.

'Come on, slowpoke,' Green admonished. 'What yu standin' around with yore mouth open for?'

Philadelphia's reply was extremely unflattering, and Green grinned. 'Yo're learnin' more than I figgered,' he told Philadelphia. 'Let's ride. That back-shootin' hombre mighta just been boogered enough to leave a trail we can follow.'

CHAPTER FIVE

FOR several miles Green was able to follow the trail he had selected without difficulty. The tracks of the horse which had been tethered to the tree behind the hillock were clear; Green noted that the would-be assassin had headed south without making any attempt to conceal his passage. Drawing rein as he and Philadelphia crested a slight ridge, he scanned the country ahead of them. Down below them, perhaps a mile away, he could see the dark line of trees and the faint silvery glint of water which marked the course of the Yavapai. Off to the east the white scar which was the trail running from the Sabre to the Mesquites could be faintly descried, and Green pointed it out to his companion.

'I'm bettin' our friend aimed like an arrow for that,' he told Philadelphia. 'Be mighty hard to track anythin' once it hit that trail.'

Philadelphia nodded glumly. 'I reckon we might as well turn back,' he said, the slump of his shoulders ample evidence of his disappointment.

'Hold hard, there,' Green told him. 'Let's mosey down an' take a look at the river-bank. Mebbe Mr. Bushwhacker crossed the river an' maybe he didn't. If he did, he might just 'a been careless about it.'

They moved down the slope from the ridge, threaded a long arroyo, and found themselves on flat, open scrubland. The trail lay off to their left, and within a few more minutes it cut diagonally across their path. When they reached it Green dismounted and spent long minutes studying the churned, sandy earth. Remounting, he shook his head. 'Impossible,' he told the youngster. 'Let's head on down to the river.'

Where the trail actually met the river, the Yavapai ran wide and shallow, with broad sandy banks sloping gently to the water.

'She's a natural ford,' Green told his friend. Tethering Nigger, he squatted down and inspected the various tracks which had been made in the sand, his keen eyes narrowed. Slowly, he moved carefully, about a foot at a time, away from the centre of the crossing towards its outer edge.

Philadelphia watched him in wonder. The edge of the river was, to his unaccustomed eyes, a morass of churned hoof-marks, some made by cattle, others by horses, and for all he knew, a few made by wild animals which might use this shallow part of the river as a watering hole.

'Jim, how could yu tell one o' the hoof-marks yo're lookin' for if yu seen it?' he asked.

Green, still carefully inspecting the ground, looked up briefly and grinned. 'There's an easy way, if she works,' he told his companion. 'Yu think about it a minnit or two.'

Philadelphia frowned. Surely, unless the horse had some special kind of shoes, any horse track would look like any other? He said as much. Green refrained from answering, but instead rose to his feet and announced, 'He crossed the river here.'

The boy looked at him in sheer amazement. 'I expect yo're goin' to describe him to me as well,' he said, disbelief in his voice.

Green shook his head. 'Might be able to, but I won't,' he said. 'Come an' take a look for yoreself.' He pointed to the hoof-mark he had been studying. 'What d'yu see?'

Philadelphia shrugged. 'Just another hoof-mark.'

'Naw,' Green persisted. 'You're lookin' but yu ain't seein'. Take a closer gander.'

The boy kneeled down and peered closely at the track. Now, this close, he could see clinging to the wet sides of the hoof-mark a few dark flecks. Picking them off with a fingernail he inspected them, then laughed.

'Pine needles,' he said, standing up. 'I'm apologisin',

Jim. Although I still don't know how yu can say it's our man.'

'Wrong again,' Green told him. 'If that track had been here since yesterday it would'a' soaked up moisture from the ground. Them pine needles is still dry. It ain't conclusive, but it's enough. Let's cross the river.'

Philadelphia hesitated. 'That's Sabre land over there, ain't it?'

'It ain't Californey, that's for shore,' grinned Green, mounting his horse and leading the way down to the water. 'Come on, Philadelphia. Let's see what that sign over there says.'

They splashed across the muddy Yavapai and trotted up the opposite bank to where a stark, sun-bleached board bore a faded legend in red paint.

THIS IS SABRE LAND

If you haven't been invited
turn around.

The Sabre brand was burned on to the wood below this unfriendly message. Green grinned over his shoulder. 'Friendly cuss, this Gunnison feller.'

Without apparently bothering any further to search for tracks he swung off down the trail towards the Sabre ranch. After a moment's hesitation Philadelphia spurred his horse after his friend. 'Never seen such a feller for pokin' in hornet's nests,' he muttered; but he kept his sentiments to himself as they rode along. As they crested a bluff, a horseman suddenly appeared off to their right about five hundred yards. He made no attempt to come closer, and matched his speed to the pace of the two men from the Mesquites.

'Don't put yore hands anywhere near yore gun,' Green told the youngster. 'That jasper's totin' a Winchester, an' he's pointin' it our way.'

A closer look revealed to Philadelphia that their shadow, although he appeared to be riding negligently, was, in fact, carrying a rifle ported across his saddle bow in their direction. No threatening move was made as they cantered on; the rider stayed at the same distance from them.

Presently they hove in sight of the house, down below them in a natural hollow, shaded by big cottonwoods, the limed adobe walls almost dazzlingly bright in the pale sunlight. Now their 'shadow' spurred on ahead of them, moving around in a semicircle until he reached the trail. There he reined his horse about and sat waiting, rifle trained on them casually, as they approached. He was a squat, surly-looking individual with a low forehead and unshaven jaws. As they drew within fifteen feet, he cocked the Winchester in one smooth, menacing movement. The click-clack of the action rang loudly in the stillness.

'Hold it right there,' the squat man told them. 'Shuck yore guns.'

With a nod to Philadelphia, Green unbuckled his belt and let the guns fall to the ground. The youngster followed his example and the man nodded, his jaws working on the cud of tobacco in his loose-lipped mouth.

'What's yore business?' he rasped.

'Want to talk to Gunnison,' Green informed him coolly.

'What about?'

'If yu'd do I wouldn't wanta talk to yore boss,' snapped Green.

The man's eyes gleamed in anger, and he kneed his horse forward until he was alongside the puncher. He jabbed Green with the barrel of the Winchester.

'Yu talk outa turn, mister, an' I'll blow yu four ways to onct,' he threatened. Green smiled, and half turned his body in the saddle as though to avoid the jabbing gun-barrel. With an evil smile the man jabbed again, opening his mouth to say something which died still-born as Green's hand suddenly grasped the gun-barrel and the guard realised he had let himself be lured off balance in the saddle. By the time he had done so, however, he was spilling in an untidy heap on the ground, and his former prisoner was smiling coldly down at him from behind the receiver of the Winchester.

'Well, well, how are the mighty fallen,' quoted the puncher; then, his voice cold, he ordered the man to take three steps backwards and to unbuckle his gunbelt. When the thoroughly cowed guard had complied with this order Green ordered him to get back on his horse.

'Philadelphia, get the guns,' he said to the youngster, who had sat open-mouthed at the speed with which this quiet-spoken man had turned the tables on his armed opponent.

He dismounted and passed Green's guns up to him. Buckling on his own pistol he remounted, and kept the guard unwaveringly covered as Green buckled on his own gunbelt.

'Pie like mother made,' Green told the guard. 'Yu wanta remember not to crowd yore luck. Lead on in, an' no fancy footwork. I got a nervous disposition when I'm trespassin'.'

They rode down the slope towards the house below. It was not until they were actually in the yard that anyone noticed anything untoward; then, with a roar of rage, one man turned and started to run towards the bunkhouse, obviously to get a gun, since he was not wearing a gunbelt. Green whipped the Winchester around and fired, and fired again. Two gouts of sand leaped up on both sides of the man, inches from his feet, and he froze.

'Stay put!' Green ordered him. The shots had drawn several men into the yard, and on the porch two men stood. The thickset one Green and Philadelphia recognised instantly as Dancy. The other was a tall, rangy man with cold grey eyes and iron-grey hair, dressed in unassuming range clothes. Only the air of a man accustomed to giving orders and having them obeyed set him apart.

'Yu'll be Lafe Gunnison, I'm guessin',' said Green as they rode up to the hitching-rail.

'Yu'll be dead in five seconds if yu don't throw down yore guns,' snapped the rancher. 'I'm warnin' yu, mister; I'm goin' to count five. If them guns ain't on the floor by then yu'll be ridden outa here on a rail.'

'If you was fool enough to start countin', I'm guessin' I could drop yu an' Dancy afore yu got to two,' Green told him levelly, and as the old man's mouth opened for another tirade he continued, 'If yu'll lissen for a moment instead o' makin' war talk yu might find I got somethin' worth yore hearin'.'

Gunnison's mouth closed like a trap. He was not

accustomed to being addressed in this manner, but neither was he fool enough to chance calling this sardonic young stranger's bluff.

'All right,' he snapped. 'Speak yore piece, an' make it short.'

In even tones, and without emphasis, Green described the events which had brought them to the Yavapai, and of the tracks he had found at the edge of the river.

'What's all this got to do with Sabre?'

The speaker was a newcomer who had come out of the house as Green spoke. He was a slim young man, expensively dressed in fine broadcloth, a soft-collared shirt, and dark four-in-hand, his boots gleaming richly in the muted sunlight. The handsome face was marred only by a weak, spoiled mouth; the hands were long, as slim as a woman's, and he gave every appearance, as Philadelphia was to later remark, of 'never havin' done a hard day's work in his life'. Gunnison turned, saw who it was, then faced Green once more.

'My son Randolph,' he said by way of introduction, 'an' he's hit the nail on the head. What's it got to do with us?'

'Mister, the hombre who tried to kill the kid here shore didn't head for Yavapai,' Green said. 'Which wouldn't leave him many other places to head for in these parts.'

'Are you,' asked young Gunnison coldly, 'suggesting that he came here?'

At Green's failure to react to this question Randy Gunnison's face set, and his lips became a thin, bloodless line. He turned to his father.

'Are you,' asked young Gunnison coldly, 'suggesting tramps ride in here and all but tell you that the Sabre hires women-killers?'

These words struck a chord in the older man's mind, and anger played across his narrowed eyes.

'My son's convinced that yore nester friends are behind all the troubles in these parts, mister, an' I ain't shore he's wrong. They are, they got plenty of enemies. An' not all of 'em live on the Sabre. But yu can bite on this: Sabre don't war on women.'

'You heard what my father said,' Randy Gunnison

spat. 'He is hampered by some old-fashioned notions about hospitality and fair play, but I'm not! You're lucky you got this far without being shot down. For two cents ...'

Green's hand had moved as the younger man spoke, and there was a stunned silence as two coins chinked at Randolph Gunnison's feet, tossed there by the tall puncher.

'There's yore two cents,' snapped Green. 'What now?' His eyes were like chips of steel, and menace was instinct in his very posture.

Gunnison paled and moved a step backwards. 'Are you going to stand for this?' he squeaked to his father.

The old man looked from Green to his son nonplussed, then a look of distaste crossed his face. 'Randy, if yu don't like the heat—stay outa the kitchen. Don't skedaddle ahind o' me when someone calls yore bluff.'

'I'm no gunfighter,' Randy Gunnison said, a surly look on his sulky face.

'Then don't talk like one,' said his father shortly. 'I'm tellin' yu now, mister ...?'

'Green,' supplied the cowboy. 'The kid's called Philadelphia.'

For the first time Gunnison looked fully at the youngster; Philadelphia had been watching the proceedings from the side, unobtrusively covering his partner's flank in case any of Gunnison's men made a threatening move. As Philadelphia turned, the old rancher's face changed. He went pale, and put out a hand to steady himself against the upright of the porch. He pointed a shaky finger at Philadelphia.

'Yu, boy,' he croaked. 'What's yore name?' When the youngster told him he shook his head. 'No, yore real name.'

'Henry Sloane, sir,' Philadelphia told him. 'Why d'yu ask?'

'Just ... just for a moment, yu put me powerfully in mind o' ... someone I used to know.' The old man shook himself, as though shedding some haunting thought, and drew himself up. 'Trick o' the light, I'm guessin'. Now, yu: Green! My son mighta given yu the impression that Sabre's long on wind an' short on action. It ain't so.

What he said still goes, just like what I said when yu started jawin'. Yu ain't told me no news I want to hear. Turn around an' get off my land. Tell yore nester friend to keep his gal indoors if he ain't got anyone can take care o' her. An' don't make the mistake o' thinkin' I'm allus this lenient. Next time my men'll have orders to shoot yu or this wet-eared kid on sight. Sabe?'

Green nodded, regret in his expression. 'I'm sorry,' he told the old rancher. 'I was told yu might be a man who'd lissen to reason, but yo're so bull-headed I doubt if yu'd know good sense if it jumped up an' bit yu. No'—he held up a hand—'don't get all riled up again. We're ridin'. Afore we go, Gunnison, ponder a mite on this: if our bushwhackin' friend didn't come back to the Sabre, where'd he go?'

Wheeling his horse, the puncher spurred the big stallion out of the yard, followed closely by his young partner, leaving the old man frowning furiously. Dancy sidled over eagerly. 'Yu want me to get a couple o' the boys an' follow 'em, boss?' He leered. 'Teach 'em some manners for next time they come a-callin', mebbe?'

Gunnison turned on the big foreman with rage on his face. 'I just told them men we don't war on women,' he thundered. 'We don't send a gang o' men out to set on two, neither. When we make war, we'll do it in the open. Until I give yu any hints otherwise, yu play it that way, hear me?'

A snarl of anger crossed Dancy's face, but he replaced it with a servile sneer. 'Yo're the boss,' he told the rancher.

'Don't yu forget it none, either,' was the retort as the old man stamped into the ranchhouse. Dancy spat in the dirt and returned to his work, throwing a glance of hatred in the direction of the retreating back of his employer.

* * *

When they were out of sight of the ranch Green reined in; his companion pulled up alongside, puzzlement on his face.

'What's up, Jim?' he wanted to know.

'We didn't find out what happened to our bushwhackin' *amigo,'* Green informed him coolly. 'I reckon I'll just mosey back an' do a mite o' checkin'.'

Philadelphia regarded his friend as if he had just announced his imminent departure for the moon.

'Jim—are yu loco? They catch yu an' they'll skin yu alive an' feed yu to the buzzards.'

Green grinned. 'I ain't aimin' to be caught.'

'Then I'm comin' with yu,' announced Philadelphia resolutely.

'Oh, no, yu ain't,' Green replied with a smile. 'Yu may be learnin' fast with that six-shooter, but I ain't had time to teach yu how to "Injun" without bein' spotted. Yu stay here with the horses. When I arrive, we'll be wantin' to leave fairly pronto. Yu be ready.'

He pointed out a clump of rocks off to the left of the trail where Philadelphia could hide with the horses until his return. Then, slipping off his high-heeled boots and socks, he padded away in the direction of the ranch, leaving the unwilling Philadelphia behind. The boy watched Green's lithe, almost effortless gait as he moved across the prairie for a short while. He turned to tether the horses, and then looked again. There was no sign of Green. The cowboy had disappeared as completely as if the earth had swallowed him.

* * *

When he was within two hundred yards or so of the ranch once more, Green ducked behind a clump of brush and surveyed the area below. Off to the right of the big house as he faced it was a long, low building in which there were several tar-paper windows; a faint plume of smoke arose from the chimney. 'Bunkhouse,' he told himself, moving his gaze across the yard to another, slightly higher building. 'That'll be the stables,' he said to himself, and his keen eyes swept over the terrain between himself and his objective. A narrow gully seemed to offer the best means of approaching the stables unseen, and crouching low, moving as fast as he could, Green drew to within about twenty yards of the building. He could hear voices quite plainly within the stables; one of them was Dancy's.

'Rub him down, feed him, an' put him in the corral,'

the Sabre man was telling someone. 'An' Jack Mado's geldin', too.'

'Okay, Jim,' said the man to whom Dancy was speaking. In a moment the foreman came out of the stable, hitched at his gunbelt, and crossed the open yard towards the big house.

A quick glance about him revealed no one else in the vicinity, and Green covered the few yards remaining between him and the building at a flat run. Almost soundlessly he skirted the wall, coming to the open door which led into the corral. He lay flat on the ground, and took a quick look around the doorway. It was an old trick; a man looking at the opening would not expect a head at floor level. Green was taking a calculated risk that the man inside would not be looking at the door. Nor was he; the tall, thin horse-tender was busily rubbing down a sorrel standing in one of the stalls.

Rising noiselessly to his feet, Green moved like a shadow inside the stable and was behind the man in three swift steps. Almost instinctively the man felt Green's presence and half turned.

'Wha——' he began, when the barrel of Green's forty-five caught him solidly behind the ear, and he fell like a sack of wheat into Green's waiting arms. The cowboy dragged the man into a vacant stall and then, crooning to soothe the slightly startled sorrel, he examined the horse. He noted the sweat marks dried on the sleek flanks, and lifted the hoofs.

'Ain't no pine needles,' he said, disappointment in his voice, 'but plenty o' sand around the fetlocks. Now the question is: who's yore rider, ol' hoss?'

He spent a few more moments examining the saddle which was straddling the stall partition. There was nothing in the saddlebags to yield a clue as to its owner. The only other horse in the stable was a gelding which, from the conversation he had overheard, Green knew to belong to the man called Jack Mado. A rapid inspection of this animal revealed no sign of pine needles or sand, nor had the horse been hard used. 'Not yu, beauty,' Green murmured. 'Whoever owns that sorrel is our man.' He thought for a moment; then, nodding, he produced a Barlow knife from his pocket and spent another minute in the stall with the sorrel. With a grim smile of satisfaction he pocketed the knife.

'I'll shore know yu when I see yu again, hoss,' he told the animal. 'Yu don't look like yu go in any remuda to me.'

By this the JH man was referring to the prevalent practice of keeping a pool of horses on a ranch for the riders to draw from daily in their work. These animals were normally half-wild, hardly-broken animals. The sorrel, on the other hand, was a good horse with some breeding in him.

'Next time I see yu I hope yore owner's ridin' yu,' Green told the animal, patting its velvety muzzle. The horse whickered softly as the cowboy edged back to the door and, after a quick glance about, once more crossed the dangerous open space to the mouth of the gully he had descended.

A few minutes later he was above the crest of the hill and loping towards his rendezvous with Philadelphia.

CHAPTER SIX

Lafe Gunnison sat in silence in the sprawling, untidy living-room of the Sabre ranchhouse. Opposite him, a petulant look on his face, his son was haranguing him.

'You know damned well that those nesters are stealing our cattle,' Randy was saying. 'This nonsense about someone trying to kill Susan Harris is just some kind of trick to make us look bad. They can tell the Marshal that they even rode across here to try to reason with you. That you told them all sorts of things you never said. Think of all the kinds of lies those conniving rogues can concoct!'

The elder Gunnison remained silent. The advent of the coolly imperturbable Green had been surprisingly upsetting; the man did not have the outward appearance of a liar, although Gunnison had met plenty of men who had the most honest and open of faces, but were black-hearted villains who would have killed their own mothers for a dollar bill. He felt restive; the cowboy had probed into some area of his mind, disturbed a feeling which he had pushed out of his thoughts, and set it to plaguing him. He could not put it into words; but it was there. Meanwhile, Randy Gunnison was still talking.

'Your old-time notions of fair play are out of date, Father,' he told the old man. 'These people aren't going to be impressed or affected by notions like that. They're out to grab our range if they can. It's up to us to stop them.'

The old man looked up at his son with tired eyes. 'How come yo're so all-fired anxious about Sabre all of a sudden?' he wanted to know. 'I ain't seen yu spendin' yore time tryin' to find out how the place is run. I figgered yu was more interested in runnin' up a bill at Tyler's, or whatever yu do with yore time.'

His son chose to ignore this familiar attack upon himself. It was an old bone of contention between them and he did not want to become side-tracked by it now.

'Never mind that now,' he told his father. 'You just remember what I say. If you give those homesteaders an inch they'll take more than a mile—they'll steal the Sabre from right under your nose! Why you've never taken the men up there and cleaned them out I'll never understand.'

'Is that what they teach you in them fancy Eastern schools I sent yu to?' growled Lafe Gunnison. 'Right is might?'

'No, Father,' Randy replied. 'They don't teach it, but you learn it just the same. All those boys in that school had parents who could buy and sell Sabre fifty times a day for a year and never notice they'd spent money. They didn't stick to the letter of the law, believe me. When the law got in their way they changed the law.'

'Damned if I don't think that sendin' yu there was the worst thing I ever done. Ever since yu come back here, yu been spoutin' about money bein' the only thing in the world worth havin'.'

'Not money, my dear father,' sneered Randy. 'Power! Money is power! You don't seem to realise that. You could brush those damned thieves in the Mesquites off you like a man swatting flies, and nobody would say a word and you know it.'

'Mebbe that's why I ain't done it, boy,' said Gunnison heavily. 'Another thing about power is the way yu use it.'

'Well, things would be very different if I were running the Sabre, I'll tell you that!' his son told him.

The old man turned, a flash of anger brightening his eyes for an instant. 'Yu ain't runnin' Sabre yet,' he growled. 'Until yu are, yu stick to yore theories an' I'll stick to mine.'

Randolph Gunnison crossed the room and opened the door to leave. As he did, he turned, shaking his head. 'I'll never understand you,' he said, without trying to hide the contempt in his voice. He slammed the door and Gunnison heard him stamping out on to the porch and calling one of the men to fetch his horse.

Gunnison shook his grey head. 'Cuts both ways, boy,' he said sadly. His thoughts turned back in their previous path, and he reviewed again what the dark-haired cowboy, Green, had said. Someone had tried to kill Susan Harris; but for what reason? He was sure that there must be an explanation behind it. Some hunter, maybe, frightening the girl? That still didn't explain the shot which had so nearly killed the boy. That boy! In that one fleeting moment the boy had borne such an amazing resemblance to ... he shook his head. The whole thing was impossible! It was some cool plot to discredit the Sabre, to make the homesteaders appear like the injured party. He snorted. Injured party, hah! Damned nesters. The story was the same wherever they took up land. The big spreads would begin to lose beef. Nothing serious: one or two head, he thought. Nesters always reckoned that killing a beef for food wasn't theft. Crumbs from the rich man's table. Then they'd graduate to two, three head. You didn't complain: it wasn't worth it. Coyotes and wolves pulled down as many every month. But nesters were always greedy. Because you've deliberately chosen to overlook the loss of a couple of head, they start to think about stealing to sell instead of stealing to eat. Botching brands, hazing ten, twenty head down to some dusty town where no questions were asked, some anonymous buyer who'd throw them into a bunch which some drover would take up north in a trail herd to the Reservation. The Injuns weren't particular whose beef they ate; and the Army asked no questions so long as the price was right. Finally, the nesters discovered that it was easier to steal than work their land, and then you had a full-time rustling problem on your hands. He slapped his thigh. 'Dammit!' he growled to himself. He'd liked the look of Jacob Harris when he'd first met the man. It had gone against the grain when he'd discovered that Harris had filed on land up in the Mesquites, land he'd always though of as Sabre land until he'd learned at the land office that he didn't even have title to the land on which his own home stood. Harris and his neighbours had become a kind of symbol of the fact that his own easy-going good-natured way had become out of date. His cronies in Tucson had sympathised: everyone knew nesters were plain no damned good. Maybe Randy was right; maybe he ought to get the men together and clean them out of the Mesquites once and for all. It had to be one of them. Maybe even the shooting at Harris's girl had been done by one of them. He shook his head. If only a man could go up there and talk to them. But no self-respecting cattleman could countenance that. Sabre was in the right. 'I was here first,' he told himself. 'Damme if I go to Harris an' apologise for it!'

He stoked an old briar pipe and sat for a long time, smoking in the silent room. There had to be something he could do. Finally, moving like a very tired man, he came to a decision and, crossing the room, he sat down at his battered old roll-topped desk. He sat there for a long moment, then pulled out a pen and some paper. Slowly, chewing the pen between words, he began to compose a letter.

CHAPTER SEVEN

THE man rode into Yavapai from the south at about noon. He was not a big man by frontier standards; perhaps five feet seven or eight, but there was strength in the supple frame. The man rode a bay stallion with an ornate Mexican saddle, decorated with silver that gleamed in the golden sunlight. Although his clothes were dusty they were evidently of good material; he did not look like a man who had ridden from Tucson within the last two days, but he had. The man on horseback entered Yavapai from the south, noting the location of the buildings in the town, a faint sneer playing about his lips.

In truth, Yavapai was nothing to look at. It was typical of any hundred other southwestern settlements of that time; a wide strip of wheel-rutted, hoof-pounded dust comprising its only street, flanked on either side by jagged rows of crude buildings, some of adobe, squat and unattractive, the two-foot-thick walls robbing them of any grace. One or two of the edifices along the street were of timber, warped and bleached by the blazing Arizona sun. A few, like the bank and Tyler's saloon, had glass windows with blinds which could be drawn to give at least an air of coolness in the midday heat. Along the street on both sides ran a boardwalk for pedestrians; it was broken here and there, and unrepaired. A few of the larger buildings boasted hitching-rails, and an attempt had been made to sweep the ever-present tin cans and bottles into piles of trash which would be collected if the town ever became civic-minded enough to care. On this inspection the stranger thought it unlikely. Yavapai appeared to have been thrown down from above haphazardly into the middle of the narrow end of the valley watered by the river from which the town took its name. Yavapai had no beauty, no charm. It had begun as a crossroads and a saloon. The store, the bank, the land office, Mrs. Robinson's restaurant had all come later and existed only to serve the cattlemen from the surrounding area: Sabre on the north, and two large spreads which lay some forty miles to the south, halfway along the road to Tucson.

The stranger spotted the bleached sign on the false front of Tyler's saloon and guided his stallion towards it. Dismounting, he hitched the animal to the rail outside and, mounting the boarded sidewalk, pushed his way through the batwing doors into the gloomy coolness of the saloon. His step was light and wary, and his right hand rarely swung more than three or four inches away from the tied-down holster at his side. The holster was an unusual one; unlike most it was a one-piece construction, an expensive gun rig in which the holster and belt had been cut entirely from the same piece of leather. The belt was, like the man's saddle, studded with silver. The holster was hand-stitched and reinforced, with a deep cut-away section carefully shaped to expose the maximum amount of butt, trigger guard, and trigger for an exceptionally fast and easy draw.

The stranger's wary gait and his ornate gunbelt could hardly have escaped the notice of the few solitaire-and-whisky cases who were in the saloon this early in the day. These few stared in speculation as the man approached the bar. He favoured them with a fleeting, narrow-eyed glance and then ignored them. Tyler came bustling along to serve the newcomer. His bonhomie fell away like autumn leaves as he looked into the cold green eyes.

'Whisky,' snapped the man. 'Pronto!' Tyler hastened to obey the curt command, pouring a generous drink into the shotglass with a slightly shaking hand. He was about to cork the bottle when the stranger laid a hand firmly on his arm and said, 'Leave the bottle. I ain't gonna be able to stomach this town without a few drinks. Gawd! What a hole!'

Tyler edged away, and busied himself polishing glasses to an unaccustomed lustre which would have startled any regular drinker in Yavapai's only saloon. The few patrons of the establishment, after their initial covert survey of the newcomer, had gone back to their drinks, their cards, and their murmured conversation.

'Yu!'

Tyler's head jerked up from his polishing as the

stranger's cold voice broke the near-silence. 'Me? Yessir, what can I do for you?'

'Mighty little, if this is yore best likker,' snapped the stranger. 'This burg got a Marshal?'

Tyler nodded. 'Name's Appleby.'

'Go get him,' commanded the stranger.

Tyler nodded unquestioningly, and hastened out of the building. As the bartender's footsteps receded, the stranger turned and hooked his elbows on the bar. He eyed the citizens of Yavapai with an expression of infinite distaste on his face.

'Get the hell outa here!' he told them. 'Move!'

Wide eyed, the half dozen men in the bar, stumbling into chairs and bumping each other in their rush to comply with this narrow-eyed stranger's command, hastened out into the sunlit street. They foregathered on the porch of the saloon, and the man inside smiled to himself as he heard their muted protests at this treatment. 'Sheep!' he said, pouring himself another drink. He tossed it down as Tyler and Tom Appleby came in through the batwing doors, affecting not to notice the fact that Appleby remained near the wall, thus leaving no opportunity for the man in the saloon to hold him silhouetted against the bright sunlight outside.

'Yo're a careful man, Marshal,' said the stranger.

'I got to be,' was the cool reply. Appleby surveyed Tyler's customer. The excited saloon-keeper had come rushing into Appleby's office gabbling about a man coming into the saloon, looking as deadly as a tarantula, apparently spoiling for trouble. What he saw was a shortish man of about thirty, with a fancy gun rig and an expression of disdain that looked as though it might be the man's permanent expression.

'So yo're the Marshal,' the man said.

'I'm the Marshal. Name's Appleby.'

'Marshal, I ast yu to come over so I could introduce myself proper. I didn't want to give the impression I was huntin' yu up.'

'All right,' Appleby said shortly. 'Yu made yore point.'

'I'm Wesley Cameron, Marshal,' the man said.

A collective gasp escaped the lips of the knot of onlookers clustered outside the saloon. The news of their summary ejection by the stranger had spread quickly, and perhaps thirty men were now gathered on the sidewalk, craning their necks to see what was going on inside.

'It's Wes Cameron,' the oldster nearest the door announced to the others in an awed voice, and the name was passed in a whisper around the group as they craned their necks even harder to catch a glimpse of this cold-faced stranger, owner of a name to strike a chill into the most hardened of hearts. Wesley Cameron! Few present had not heard the name. The man was a walking legend, one of the breed that had included Hickok and Billy the Kid and Johnny Hardin. Cameron, it was said, had cleaned up Galeyville, had been on the losing side in the Lincoln County troubles, and had won a reputation as a cold-blooded killer in the Texas Salt Wars. He was always just on the right side of the law, was said to have always given his man an even break. It was also rumoured—although no one had ever dared to voice the rumour in Cameron's presence—that he was a hired gun, one of that bloodless breed who would, for pay, force another man into a situation which could only be resolved by gunplay. All of this, and more, was part of the gabble of whispering that circulated in the crowd outside Tyler's as Tom Appleby digested this news.

'I've heard o' yu,' the Marshal told the newcomer. 'What do yu want with me?'

'Just declarin' myself, Marshal,' Cameron said with a wolfish smile. 'I'm aimin' to spend a while in yore delightful mee-tropolis, an' I wanted to start off right.' Appleby nodded, and Cameron continued. 'I'm a peaceful hombre, Marshal, an' I ain't huntin' no trouble.' He spread his hands. 'But yu know how it is. I turn up someplace, an' some damn' fool has to try an' find out if I'm as fast as they say.'

'Yu ain't likely to run into that kind o' trouble here,' Appleby said levelly.

'I shore hope not,' Cameron said. His smile was nearly sincere as he added, 'But just in case ... well, I been in some towns where the Law warn't exactly ... impartial.'

'Cameron,' the Marshal said. 'Yu'll get the same treatment in Yavapai that any peaceable citizen gets—as long as yu stay peaceable. If there's any trouble——' He pointed a finger at Cameron's pearl-handled revolver. 'Yu better have a good reason for bein' in it! Yu step out o' line an' I'll have to take yu in.'

'Hell, Marshal,' Cameron smiled, the wolfish expression back on his face, 'I'd hate that. I ain't never killed a Marshal yet.'

The insult hovered in the air, bait waiting to be taken; but the Marshal did not rise to it.

'How long yu figger to stay?' he asked.

'Long as it takes.'

'Yu mind tellin' me yore business here?'

'Shore do.' The reply was flat and cold and Cameron's manner was baitingly watchful. Appleby, however, just shrugged.

'Yore business,' was all he said. 'But remember what I said: yu pull one more stunt like treein' Tyler's saloon an' I'll run yu in.'

Cameron nodded, a faint smile lingering about his lips. 'Just wanted a mite o' privacy, Marshal,' he said. Raising his voice he called out, 'Hey! Yu gents out there come on in! I'm buyin' drinks for everyone! Come on, come on in!'

The crowd outside looked at each other for reassurance, and those in front shuffled their feet hesitantly as the gunman repeated his invitation, louder this time. One man, bolder than the rest, pushed in through the doors, and then, slowly, the others followed, almost mesmerised by the fact that the famous, the infamous Wes Cameron was here in Yavapai, and not only that but about to buy drinks for them all. Gradually they came sheepishly in. Cameron was as good as his word, and soon there was a sizeable knot of men standing alongside him at the bar, drinking in his words, eager to be near him, to slap his shoulder, to watch his every movement so that later they would be able to boast that they had drunk at the same bar as Wesley Cameron.

Appleby watched the crowd sourly for a moment as they clustered around the gunman, and nodded to himself. Cameron would be a ten-day wonder; the same mob would as cheerfully hang the gunman if they were given enough cause, and led to it. For some reason the thought seemed to amuse him. He smiled briefly and then turned and pushed his way out into the street. Over the heads of the clustering sycophants around him Cameron watched the Marshal leave, and a sardonic smile touched his lips. Good actor, he told himself. Wonder if he's got any nerve when the chips are down? Probably not, otherwise I wouldn't be here now. He turned back to his new 'friends' with inward distaste, forcing a smile on to his face.

CHAPTER EIGHT

SEVERAL uneventful days had passed; Green had told Harris to pass the word along to his neighbours to be double careful, after the bushwhacking attempt on Susan and the youngster. Philadelphia had been constantly plaguing the cowboy with questions about his foray on to the Sabre. What had he done? What had he seen? What had he found? To these and all the boy's queries Green turned a deaf ear. 'Yu'll know soon enough,' he told Philadelphia. 'Meanwhile, yu keep yore eyes skinned for anyone pokin' around these parts who don't belong up here.'

Indeed, the cowboy was in no mood for questions. He was himself unable to properly explain what he had discovered on the Sabre. It appeared that someone on the ranch was responsible for the attempt on Philadelphia's life, but it seemed very unlikely that Lafe Gunnison knew about it. The man was bluff and forthright; he was not the kind of actor who could carry off a deception of such magnitude, Green was convinced. If Gunnison was ignorant of the fact that someone in his employ was responsible for the ambush, then it followed that the motive which could have been attributed to the bushwhacker—that he was working for Gunnison, trying to throw a scare into Harris in order to make the homesteader move off his land—no longer applied. That being so, what was the motive? Why had Philadelphia and the girl been fired on? These and other thoughts occupied the puncher's mind as he went about his daily tasks until in the end he revealed them to Harris.

'Yo're sayin' that Gunnison don't know someone on his ranch tried to kill my gal?' the homesteader asked.

Green nodded. 'Can't rightly figger it out,' he said. 'She don't make sense. Unless there's some other reason for gettin' yu off this land that ain't got nothin' to do with Gunnison...?'

The old man shook his head. 'Beats me, Jim. This land just don't seem worth all the trouble.'

'Tell me about when yu first come here, Jake,' suggested Green. 'It might just give me some ideas.'

'Not much to tell,' the homesteader told him. 'Reb Johnstone an' Stan Newley was the first to file on land up here. When I came out from Missouri it seemed a likely thing to file alongside 'em. Kitson came next, then Taylor.'

'How long ago was all this?' the cowboy wanted to know.

'Gettin' on three, four years now,' Harris told him. 'Reb's been here longest: just over four years.'

'Yu all built yore own places?'

Harris nodded. 'No, wait a minnit,' he corrected himself. 'Reb Johnstone moved into an old cabin when he first come up here. His place stands where the cabin used to be. Some kind o' line shack, I think it was.'

Green nodded again. 'This trouble—the raids, the horse-stealin' that Kitson mentioned: when did all that start?'

'Oh ... mebbe eighteen months ago, more or less. Difficult to say, exactly. Never took notice at first: figgered it was just wanderin' bucks liftin' a few o' Terry's hosses. On'y got wise to it when it kept on happenin'. When Reb Johnstone an' Stan Newley had night riders on their land we knew it warn't no accident.'

'An' Gunnison started complainin' about losin' beef around the same time?'

The homesteader looked at Green for a long moment, a light dawning in his eyes. 'I'm beginnin' to get yore drift, Jim,' he said. 'Yo're figgerin' mebbe the same outfit's behind the whole thing?'

'Could be,' Green told him, 'but who? If it ain't

Gunnison, an' it ain't any o' yore people—who is it?'

The homesteader shook his head. 'I keep goin' around in the same tracks yu do, Jim, an' I keep comin' up with the same answer: I dunno.'

The old man poked a twig into the flickering fire and lit an old black pipe with the brand. He puffed away in silence for a while, looking reflectively into the flames.

'Jim,' he began hesitantly. 'We ain't talked much, yu an' me.'

The puncher nodded, not speaking.

'I got the feelin' there's somethin' yu wanted to tell me,' Harris said. 'Yu reckon now might be a good time for it?'

Green looked at the old homesteader for a long moment and then a bitter look crossed his face. 'Yo're better off not knowin',' he said harshly.

'Never figgered exactly why a feller like yu would want to work for a farmer,' Harris continued imperturbably. 'Yo're a top hand, Jim. Yu coulda got good wages on any spread in Arizona. Yet yu come here. Why?'

'I heard down in Tucson that there was some tough hombres gatherin' in these parts,' Green told him. 'I figgered mebbe the men I'm lookin' for might be in Yavapai.' Harris looked his interest, and the cowboy continued, 'Their names is Webb an' Peterson. Yu ever run across them?'

'Can't say I have,' Harris admitted. 'What yu want 'em for?'

'They've lived too long,' Green said, and there was a deadly coldness in his words that sent a chill across the rancher's heart.

'Yu ain't on the dodge, Jim?'

Green shook his head. 'Yu better hear the whole story, Jake,' he told his employer. 'Yu know me as Jim Green, but back in Texas they call me Sudden.'

Sudden! Jake Harris looked as if for the first time at this quietly spoken man who sat beside him. So this was the daredevil whose exploits were a legend, the man whose speed with a six-gun was talked about with bated breath wherever men spoke low over a game of cards or a drink. Sudden, who had cleaned out Hell City! * Harris

* Related in *Sudden Rides Again* (Corgi Books).

had heard about his lightning speed on the draw, his amazing adventures. And a chord in his memory told him that Sudden was wanted for murder. 'Yu said yu wasn't on the dodge,' he pointed out. His voice was mild, but Green did not miss the reproachful note.

'I ain't wanted in Arizona,' he told Harris. 'An' I never even seen the man they're huntin' me for killin' in Texas.' His words were biting, compelling. Harris sat in astounded silence as the black-haired cowboy outlined the story of his past, the chain of events in which mere chance had resulted in his becoming the legendary gunfighter called Sudden, and how he had come by the unenviable reputation he owned. With only an occasional exclamation Harris heard of a boy's promise to a dying man, of a never-ending search for two murderers named Peterson and Webb. In uncompromising phrases the cowboy told his employer of the false accusation which had resulted in his being outlawed, sent alone into the endless West, a price on his head and every man's hand turned against him.* At the end of the story Harris shook his head.

'Jim, I never heard anythin' like it,' he confessed. 'But I'm believin' yu right down the line! If yo're Sudden, then there's been a pack o' damned lies told about yu!'

'I'm obliged, seh,' was Green's grateful reply. 'I'm thinkin' it might be better if yu keep it to yoreself for the time bein'. No need to advertise it: it might come back on yu, hirin' a notorious gunfighter.'

His words were bitter, and the old man rose and clapped him on the shoulder.

'If there's real trouble I can't think of a man I'd rather have alongside me,' he said. 'I'm behind yu all the way, an' billy-be-damned to anyone as don't like it. But if yu want to play her that way, what yu say goes, Jim.'

Green smiled; his employer's confidence in him was a rewarding thing. 'Yu won't regret it, Jake,' he said.

'I ain't figgerin' to,' Harris rumbled. 'Yu got any idea how to get to the bottom o' these troubles we been rakin' over, Jim?'

'One or two,' Green told him. 'I'd like to disappear for a few days. Like to poke around, ask a few questions.

* Related in *Sudden—Outlawed* (Corgi Books).

Would yu cover for me if anyone asks where I'm at? Tell 'em I've gone up into the Yavapais to see if I can get a line on the rustlers.'

'Yu ain't meanin' our people, too, Jim?' Harris was shocked, but Sudden's voice was grim as he replied:

'Until we know for shore who's behind these troubles, I ain't shore yu oughta confide in anyone, Jake. Let's make her yore secret an' mine until I've had a chance to look around in peace. After that, we might have a line we can follow.'

Harris looked dubious, but he nodded. 'Whatever yu say, Jim.' He knocked out the dottle from his pipe into the fireplace, asking, 'When d'yu figger to leave?'

'First light,' Green said. 'An' don't let Philadelphia foller me. I aim to travel far an' fast.'

With this final injunction he bade his employer good-night. The homesteader filled his pipe again, lighting it by the same method as before. Leaning in his chair, he watched the smoke drifting upwards, his face thoughtful. Remarkable though the black-haired cowboy's revelation had been, he did not for a moment entertain any doubt that every word of it was true. 'Driftin',' he told himself. 'An' driftin' the wrong way. I just knowed he warn't no ordinary puncher. I'm durned glad I ain't the Sheriff who's lookin' for him: I'd hate to find him, if he didn't want to be found.'

CHAPTER NINE

RIVERTON, the next town south of Yavapai on the trail to Tucson, was almost a carbon copy of its northern neighbour. The dirt street, the straggle of buildings of timber, 'dobe, or mixtures of both were different only in the signs on them. In Riverton's street the dust was hock-deep, and a stiff westerly breeze tossed handfuls of it into the eyes of pedestrians hurrying about their business. Unlike Yavapai, Riverton boasted no bank, and its only eating place was a hash-house run by a wooden-legged ex-cowboy named Casey, who had been trampled in a stampede many years earlier and, after a few years as a trail cook, had decided to go into business for himself. His food was eatable; nothing more. The lack of competition kept him busy, and at around one o'clock in the afternoon he was usually able to stand with his greasy hands on his ample hips and count a satisfactory full house. He was doing this very thing when the stranger came in, and he bent his full attention upon the newcomer. Tall, but stooped as though his shoulders bore some heavy weight, the man was dressed in cheap Levi's, a woollen shirt that looked as if it had been cast off in the War Between the States, and cracked, battered boots without spurs. He wore no gunbelt, but Casey could see the butt of what looked like an old cap and ball revolver protruding from the man's trouser waistband. The man removed a grease-stained old sombrero from his head, revealing hair matted with dirt and sand, and whose colour might once have been dark brown or black. Steel-rimmed eyeglasses and a heavy stubble of beard adorned the face, and when the newcomer smiled sheepishly at him and took a seat at a table Casey noted that the man's teeth were stained and yellow. Casey was a great one for taking note of his customers' personal appearance. He had several times, when he first opened for business, made the mistake of serving panhandlers like this one only to find, after they had consumed his food, that they had no money. He had extracted his price from their faces with his own meaty fists, but it wasn't the same. He had vowed therefore to make sure which of his customers could pay before he served them. Casey stumped over to where the man had taken his seat, and the man cringed at his approach.

'Good ... good day to you, sir,' he mumbled. 'I'd ... I'd like ...'

'Afore yu tell me what yu'd like, let's see the colour of yer money,' Casey told him peremptorily. 'This ain't no charity I'm runnin'.'

One or two of his regular customers grinned. Casey's preference for cash on the barrel was well known in Riverton; they watched, half hoping that the nondescript newcomer would have no money, for Casey would surely thereupon provide an entertaining few minutes before the penurious one was thrown into the dusty street. They were disappointed, however; the man produced a greasy buckskin sack, and showed Casey a dollar bill—creased and battered almost beyond recognition, but a dollar it surely was. Casey nodded and, returning to his kitchen, dished up the meal. He thereupon forgot about the man, as customers finished their meals, and paid; others entered and ordered. Around the middle of the day was always busy, and it was not until about two-thirty that the wooden-legged hash-slinger noticed that the stranger who'd paid with the ragged dollar bill was still in his chair, smoking a vile-smelling cigar. He stumped across the room, now empty except for the smoking one, and stood facing him, arms akimbo.

'Yu've finished.' It was not a question, and the man nodded nervously. 'Yu'll be leavin', then.' The man nodded again.

He rose to go, and then hesitantly stuttered, 'Mi-might I ask yore help, mister?'

'If it's money yu want, the answer's no,' Casey told him flatly.

The stranger shook his matted head. 'No ... heh, heh ... not money, got plenty o' money. Well ... as good as money.' He tapped the side of his nose and winked at Casey knowingly, while that worthy maintained his outward air of puzzled indifference.

'What's yore name, mister?' Casey barked.

'Name's Smith,' the man told him. 'John Smith.' His cracked smile was evil, and the stink of liquor on his breath was strong enough to cut with a carving knife. 'Yu reckon I could find me a buyer for some cows I got?'

'How many head?' Casey wanted to know. 'An' what's the brand?'

'Fifty,' replied the man who had called himself Smith. 'As to the brand ... heh, heh, heh ... it's the Variable brand ... heh, the Variable.' He spluttered and wheezed as though these words were mountainously funny, while Casey regarded him stonily.

'What makes yu think I can help yu find a buyer?' he snapped. 'I ain't in the cattle business.'

'Never said yu was,' cackled Smith. 'If yu don't know

nobody, no harm done.... I'll be off to the saloon, then.'

Casey watched the man leave his premises, and waited until Smith had loped across the street and into Buckmaster's Long Branch saloon. Then, with surprising speed, the hash-handler doffed his apron, clapped a stetson on his bald pate, and quit his establishment, following a route which led him around the back of the houses on the east side of the street to an alley shaded by a tall cottonwood. He knocked on a heavy timber door, and a cold voice said, 'Who is it?'

'Casey,' puffed the old man, winded by his effort in the afternoon sun. The door opened, and a cold-eyed man in a dark suit bade him enter.

* * *

John Smith sat in the rear of Buckmaster's saloon nursing his drink. From beneath the forward-tilted brim of his battered stetson he watched the flow of customers in and out of the saloon with keen eyes. At this time of day there were not many faces to watch, but he kept on guard none the less. A faint smile, completely out of character with the cackling, dirty character who had spoken to Casey, crossed his face. 'If Philadelphia seen me now,' he murmured, 'he'd probably say I was loco—an' I ain't shore but he'd be right.' Sudden—for such was the identity of the itinerant who had so completely foxed the hash-handler—saw no signs that his very broad hints of stolen cattle for disposal had been directed at the right man, but it seemed obvious that someone who had contact with practically every visitor to the town would know what Green wanted to know. This was his reason for coming to Riverton. He had asked Harris for some old and battered clothes, ignoring the older man's curious stare, and, shortly prior to entering Riverton, had rubbed sand and earth sparingly into his hair to give it a tangled, matted effect. Unshaven jaws had also been rubbed with earth to heighten the look of unvarnished scruffiness, and as a finishing touch Green had found the steel-rimmed glasses in the Harris house just before he had left. The result, when he altered his height by stooping, stained his teeth by chewing tobacco, and swilling whisky round his mouth to make his breath stink of liquor, and changed his normally lithe walk by replacing it with a lop-sided loping gait, was a complete transformation of his appearance.

'Mightn't be necessary a-tall,' he had told himself. 'But it'd be a mite unfortunate if anyone in Riverton reckernised me.'

As he sat at the table thinking, he saw two men come in, and his eyes narrowed. They let their gaze wander, apparently with only the mildest interest, about the saloon, not remaining on him any longer than anyone else there. One of the two men was a tall, cadaverous-looking individual with a wide-brimmed, flat-crowned white hat such as those worn by plantation owners. The appearance of a rich Southern landowner was heightened by the dark suit, the brocaded waistcoat, and the shining knee-boots, worn without spurs. The man was trimming a long panatella cigar, and Sudden heard him order bourbon whisky with branch water. 'Riverboat gambler,' was Green's guess as he bent his attention upon the man's crony. This one was almost uncomfortably fat, and perspiration lay upon his face like melting lard. The man stood no more than five feet high, and was almost as wide across the middle. He wore only white linen shirt and trousers, and a pair of flat-heeled half-boots. Around his enormous middle hung a gunbelt. As far as the cowpuncher could see, the gambler was unarmed, but he bet himself the man would have a hideaway gun somewhere on his person.

'Shore looks the type,' he told himself. 'Wal, here goes!'

So saying, he rose to his feet, assuming once more the half-crouched gait of the John Smith whose role he was playing, and approached the bar. He ordered beer, and stood next to the tall gambler to drink it.

'Mighty hot today, ain't it?' offered the fat man, mopping his face with a large white bandanna. Sudden nodded, smiling weakly.

'Kind o' weather makes a man wish he didn't have to work for a livin',' pursued the fat man.

'Know ... know what yu mean,' grinned Green

fatuously. 'Feel the same way. Yu gents care to set down, jine me fer a snort?'

'Don't mind if I do,' agreed the fat man. 'Rance?' He turned to his companion, who affected to notice 'John Smith' for the first time.

'Ah beg yo' pardon?'

'This gent's invitin' yu to jine him,' the fat man said.

'Ah don't b'lieve Ah've had the pleasure, suh?' the man named Rance said to Green. Green introduced himself as John Smith, and the man nodded and, dusting the seat with a handkerchief, sat down at the table.

'What business yu in, Mr. Smith?' asked the fat man.

'Heh ... this 'n' that,' Green mumbled. 'Sellin' an' buyin'.'

'An' what brings yu-all to Riverton, Mr. Smith,' asked the gambler silkily, '—buyin' or sellin'?'

Green smiled. 'S-sell ... say: yu boys ain't the Law, or anythin'? I mean ...'

The fat man held up a deprecating hand. 'My dear feller,' he said. 'Thisyere if Rance Fontaine. He's one o' the biggest businessmen in these parts. Runs a ranch up north o' here.'

'Ah'm shoah Mr. Smith heah didn't come to talk about me,' said Fontaine. His voice changed, became businesslike and sharp. 'Who told yu to come here, Smith?'

Sudden smiled grimly to himself at the disappearance of Fontaine's pose, although no trace of his satisfaction appeared on his face, which was, to the watchers, a study in confusion and nervousness.

'Why ... I ... yu ... I was told ...' he stuttered, apparently almost frightened out of his wits.

'Who told yu, Smith?' snarled the fat man, leaning forward. In the same moment Sudden felt a solid poke in the ribs, and knew that the fat man had drawn his gun under the concealment of his huge midriff, and that the barrel was now flush against his, Sudden's, heart.

'Yu ... yu gents got me ... heh, heh ... all wrong,' he managed. 'I done heard a feller could offload a few head ... down here. Nobody mentioned no names. I just ... I just heard it. In a saloon ... Tyler's, I think it was called.'

'Where'd yu get the cattle?' snapped the fat man. His

former bumbling appearance had dropped away. Green mentally saluted him for his acting ability; he imagined very few people in Riverton paid more than passing attention to this perspiring fat man, yet it was plain to see he was as dangerous as a cornered pack-rat.

'Picked ... picked 'em up in a canyon up in the Yavapais,' he said. 'I was ... I was just prospectin' up there, tryin' to raise a few ounces o' dust. Hoss broke his hobbles an' I ... had to track him down. Found him in this box canyon.'

'Where d'yu say this was?' the fat man demanded.

'Up in the Yavapais, northeast o' Apache Canyon,' Green told them.

'An' yu say yu found the cattle in this canyon?'

'Yeah,' Green told them. 'Couldn't unnerstand it. Nobody around. No riders. Yet these cows all bunched in the one canyon. I figgered somebody had rounded 'em up ... mighty kind, heh, heh, I figgered. I hazed 'em along the river-bank, movin' at night. Never seen a soul the whole time I was in that country.'

The fat man looked at his colleague, and that worthy jerked his head. 'Stay put,' the fat man told Green, and rose to walk off a few yards away from the table. Green covertly watched their expressions. The tall man was telling the shorter one that there was something peculiar about the story they had been told; the fat man kept shaking his head and sneering.

'Rance Fontaine b'lieves my story the way I b'lieve his,' Green told himself. 'Let's hope Fatty there persuades him.' It seemed as though his hopes were to be realised, for a moment later the two men returned to the table.

'Where's the herd, Smith?' asked the fat man.

'In a safe place,' replied Sudden, putting a fatuous smile on his face. 'I got 'em cached tight.'

They dickered for a few moments about prices, and agreed on a figure. The tall Fontaine stood up. 'Vince here'll make arrangements about payin' yu,' he said. He turned on his heel and walked away without another word.

'He ... ain't too perlite,' said Green surlily, playing his part. Vince's smile was anything but warm.

'He don't have to be,' he told Green. 'Now where'd yu say yu got yore camp?'

Green gave him directions for getting to a watering hole that he had passed, north of town, and told him he would wait for him there.

'I'll be along at nightfall,' Vince promised him. 'Yu be keerful with that shootin' arn o' yourn, Smith. I don't aim to get shot by no nervous cow-thief.'

Sudden nodded, maintaining his nervous pose until the fat man finally bade him farewell and left the saloon. The man from the Mesquites moved apparently carelessly across the room as Vince crossed the street. Through a window he was able to pinpoint the man's path and notice that he disappeared up an alley farther up the street. Green nodded once and then shuffled out of the back door of the saloon. Behind one of the houses he had tethered Nigger, and in his saddlebags were stowed his own clothes and guns. Dousing himself quickly with water from a nearby trough, Green removed the dirt and grime from his hair and face. A few minutes later, the identity of Smith completely shed, he emerged once more into the street of Riverton, his hat pulled low over his face to avoid the million-to-one chance that someone in the town would know him.

On silent feet he slipped up the alleyway he had marked as Vince's route. The sound of hearty laughter emerging from a slightly open window drew him near; crouching, he edged to a position below the sill of the window. The voices were those of the two men he had met in the saloon.

'... money from home,' Vince was saying, to the accompaniment of gusts of laughter from Fontaine. 'The old geezer tells me where he's got the cows. I ride out there to pay him an' he hands the cows over to me.'

'On'y yu pay him in lead, 'stead o' silver,' said Fontaine. 'It's easy pickin's.'

'Ol' fool musta been born yestiddy,' laughed Vince. 'He shore oughta be put away, anyways. If Jim Dancy gets ahold o' him he'll salt his tail shore!'

'Yu don't reckon...' Once again Fontaine burst out laughing. 'Yu mean ... this ol' soak found Dancy's canyon?'

'It's gotta be, Rance,' hooted Vince. 'There couldn't be two that close to Apache Canyon.'

The two men laughed again, and the listening puncher smiled grimly to himself. His ruse had worked like a charm, better than he had dared hope. If Jim Dancy was selling these two cattle, as their conversation indicated, then he was stealing them from either Sabre or from the homesteaders. If Dancy was behind the rustling, then someone else was behind Dancy and it wasn't Lafe Gunnison, who would hardly be likely to steal his own cattle. Sudden's half-smile changed to a grim one; it looked like he was overdue a long chat with Mr. Dancy. He edged back from his listening post and swiftly walked the few yards to where he had hitched Nigger.

The idea of arranging a reception for the fat man when he went to the waterhole that night intending to kill poor, defenceless 'John Smith' occurred to him, and caused a frosty smile to play around his eyes, but he dismissed the temptation.

'There's more important things to do,' he told himself. 'I'd best head back for the Mesquites. Jake'll be wondering what's happened to me.'

CHAPTER TEN

For the tenth time that evening Jake Harris said, 'I shore as hell wish I knew where Jim was!'

Susan Harris stamped her foot with suppressed rage as her father uttered these words. 'Oh, Daddy, if you say that again I'll scream. Jim's being here wouldn't have made any difference. What happened happened; I suppose it is as well that it was no worse.'

Harris shook his head. Indeed, his daughter might be unwittingly right. If Green had been around this morning, then there might have been even worse to think about than what had happened.

He had been out in the corral when the sound of hoofs along the trail to the south had warned them of the approach of a lone rider. Accustomed now to the precautions instilled in her by her father, and also by Green, Susan Harris came to the door to meet him, his shotgun in her hands. She gave him the gun and with a worried look on her pretty face asked him where Philadelphia was.

'He's over at Taylor's,' her father told her. 'I sent him to borrow an axe from Alex. Don't fret yoreself, girl!'

Susan nodded and moved back into the shadow of the house as her father, the rifle cradled across his arm, turned to face the oncoming rider, who could now be seen loping up the trail towards the ranch.

Harris descried a man of medium height riding a very fine bay stallion. The man's saddle was lavishly ornamented with silver conchos and buckles. The man himself was a complete stranger, but Harris did not miss the peculiarly cut gun holster; this was no passer-by, he told himself. The shotgun remained at port across his arm.

The stranger reined in his horse and sat in the saddle in the centre of the yard, surveying the house and the smaller outbuildings with a sneer.

'What's yore business, mister?' called Harris. The newcomer completely ignored his challenge and continued with his disdainful survey of the place. He spat, then kneed his horse forward as Harris repeated his question.

'Yo're Harris?'

'I am. What do yu want? Who are yu?'

'Just wanted to see yu, Harris,' the man said. 'Heard a lot about yu. Yu ast my name: it's Cameron. Wes Cameron. I expect yu've heard about me, too.'

'That I have,' snapped Harris,' an' none of it good.'

'Watch yore tongue, yu ol' goat!' snapped Cameron. 'I'm just admirin' yore place, but yu push me hard an' I might alter the look of it some.'

Harris hitched the shotgun significantly forward, but the cold-eyed Cameron feigned not to notice.

'I'd guess yu was thinkin' o' leavin' these parts,' he said, as if to no one in particular. 'Wise decision. This high country looks plumb unhealthy to me for a man yore age.'

'Damn' yore eyes!' rumbled Harris. 'Yu got yore gall, mister! I'm guessin' yo're about to roll yore tail afore I perforate it.'

Cameron smiled. It was a cold, mirthless smile, and it did not touch the eyes. He dismounted and started to walk towards Jake Harris, who covered the menacing figure with the shotgun.

'Hold it right there!' he told Cameron. The gunman took no notice of the words.

In a voice that could almost have been described as teasing he said, 'Yu aim to blow me apart with that scattergun in front o' yore daughter, Harris? Yu know what a man looks like that's been shot close-to with one o' those things? Yu want yore daughter to see that?'

Jake Harris hesitated for a fateful moment, and in that moment the gunman's hand moved like a striking snake, knocking the barrel of the shotgun aside. His right hand swept to the cut-away holster and came up holding the pearl-handled six-shooter. It rose and fell, and Jake Harris dropped senseless to his knees, blood pouring from the cut behind his ear made by the viciously wielded gun-barrel. Susan Harris, seeing the murderous expression on Cameron's face as the gun-barrel was raised to strike yet again, swept back the door and threw herself at the man, her hands outstretched, fingernails reaching for the twisted face.

Cameron caught her hands easily, his grip like steel, and twisted them backwards until he held her, panting, her face only inches from his own.

'Well, now,' he leered. 'If yu ain't the wildcat! Purty, too! How about a li'l kiss, honey?'

He bent his head towards her, and the girl, struggling helplessly, tried desperately to prevent his beastly caress; half fainting, powerless in his clasp, she closed her eyes as his snarling face came nearer.... Suddenly his grip was loosed, and she collapsed, falling alongside her father. Looking up, she saw Cameron stumbling backwards as Philadelphia, who had ridden into the yard unseen and come up behind the man, yanked at Cameron's shirt collar, pulling the man backwards off balance, his arms flailing. Philadelphia turned the man half around, still off balance, and with all his strength drove a wicked uppercut to the gunman's jaw. Cameron cartwheeled backwards, sprawling in the dust of the yard. Cursing, spitting blood from his gashed mouth, he struggled to sit upright, shaking his head to clear it. Philadelphia stepped forward as Cameron got groggily to his feet and again hit the man, this time on the side of the head. Cameron went down like a pole-axed steer. The boy turned and raced to help Susan Harris, who was struggling to her feet.

Philadelphia knelt down to lift Jake Harris's head as the old man stirred, moaning feebly. Susan ran into the house and emerged with a bowl of water. Philadelphia poured it unceremoniously over the old man's face, and spluttering, Jake Harris sat up. In a few moments the light was back in his eyes, as Philadelphia assured him that Susan was perfectly safe. The girl went back into the house for more water. None of them paid any attention to the prone form of Cameron. Had they been doing so they would have seen him stir, then carefully roll his head to see where they were. A rictus of hatred contorted the man's face, and with a smooth movement, cursing as pain shot through his bruised jaw, Cameron was on his feet. At the same moment that Cameron regained his feet Susan Harris appeared in the doorway of the house, and her mouth opened in astonishment as she saw the crouched, menacing figure behind her father and Philadelphia.

Philadelphia wheeled, then halted as he saw Cameron. The gunman's smile was as inviting as death.

'Yo're careless, boy,' he told Philadelphia. 'Never turn yore back on a man 'less'n yo're shore yu've put him down for good.'

The boy's face was a study in self-disgust. He took a step forward, but Jake Harris laid a detaining hand on his arm.

'No, Philly,' he said firmly. 'That's Wes Cameron—he's a paid killer an' mighty fast. Don't yu go up agin him.'

The boy looked uncertainly from Cameron to his employer and back again.

Cameron let a wolfish smile play on his features. 'Yo're wonderin' if yo're fast enough, ain't yu, boy? Well, yu ain't ... so don't try it. I ain't in the kid-killin' business. However, I owe yu somethin'....' He fingered his swollen jaw, and his eyes were merciless. Faster than the watchers could follow, his hand darted to the cut-away holster and two shots blasted from his hip. Philadelphia reeled backwards and fell to the ground; Susan Harris screamed, and a curse exploded from her father's lips.

'Yu murderin' scum!' he ground out, his eyes moving helplessly to the shotgun lying in the dust about ten feet away.

Cameron smiled. 'He ain't dead, Harris. I just made shore he don't sneak up on me again for a few weeks.'

A closer look at the boy, beside whom Susan Harris was kneeling, showed that the gunman's shots had in fact both pierced the thick muscles of the thigh on both the boy's legs. Blood stained the youngster's bleached Levi's, but he was already sitting up, cursing weakly. Harris stared at the gunman, as if trying to divine from the man's face some secret that lay behind it. Noticing the old man's gaze, the gunman laughed.

'Yo're worryin', Harris,' he laughed. 'That's the first sensible thing yu've done since I came. Yo're thinkin' about what woulda happened if I'd come up here when yu wasn't around, or if I'd made less noise to let yu know I was comin'.' He nodded at the girl. 'She's right purty. Yu think about what I said about the climate up here. Mention it to yore neighbours. I'll be around.'

Without another word, he wheeled about and walked to his magnificent stallion. Mounting, he turned the horse's head and thundered off away from the Harris ranch, while the old homesteader looked at his daughter with stricken eyes.

* * *

The events of the day were still plaguing him as Susan bustled about, preparing new dressings for Philadelphia's wounds. After a solid hour of arguing he had agreed to allow her to nurse him only when, teeth chattering, he had been unable to argue more. The fever of shock that had followed the shooting had now abated and Philadelphia was sleeping in an adjoining room. Despite his daughter's outburst Harris still wondered where the dark-haired cowboy in whom, he realised, he had come to place such complete faith, had gone. He wanted to seek Green's slow-spoken reassurance, for the cold threats that Cameron had delivered had for once weakened the homesteader's determination never to be pushed off his land.

'It's one thing when they fight man to man,' he muttered. 'But makin' war on women ... that's no better'n Injuns.' Again he pondered the long talks he had already had with Green—he could still somehow not quite bring himself to think of his employee as 'Sudden'—about Gunnison.

'That ol' devil could be playin' a mighty clever double game,' he told himself. 'Mebbe Jim's figgerin' is too simple. Mebbe it's a whole lot deeper than we all think.' These thoughts and others like them occupied his mind as he paced the floor puffing furiously on his old pipe, a frown of concentration upon his weather-beaten face. And all the time, in his mind's eye, he saw the sneering face of Wes Cameron, and heard the unspoken threats the man had made upon Susan. The reputation that was Cameron's was such that the old man wondered whether even Sudden, whose speed on the draw was said to be lightning fast, could match it.

'He's the on'y hope I got,' the old man told himself; but there was a touch of resignation, a hint of defeat in his voice as he said it.

CHAPTER ELEVEN

SUDDEN arrived back at the JH on the morning after Cameron's visit and its aftermath. Stunned by the events which the old homesteader recounted, the puncher listened in silence as Jake told him of Cameron's thinly veiled threats.

'Mebbe we ought to send Miss Susan away, at that,' he said thoughtfully, but that young lady tossed her head spiritedly in dismissal of such a suggestion.

'This is my home, and no thug with a gun is going to frighten me away,' she said calmly. 'Jim, Daddy, I appreciate your concern. But I'm not going. Anyway,' she added in a lighter voice, 'who'd look after our invalid?'

Green went into the little bedroom where Philadelphia lay. The fever had paled the youngster's complexion, and he looked startlingly like the thin-faced tenderfoot who had so nearly been the victim of Jim Dancy's liquor rage that day in Yavapai.

'Yu shore got the easy life,' Sudden told him with a smile. 'Pretty nurse, good food, an' no work.'

Philadelphia smiled ruefully. 'Any time yu wanta change places, Jim, speak up,' he said. 'I'd give a couple o' years' pay to be able to go out huntin' for that coyote Cameron.'

'Yu take yore medicine,' Sudden told him. 'Cameron'll keep. There's bigger fish fryin' in these parts. Get yoreself fit: I'll be needin' yu.'

'Yu bet, Jim,' said the boy, his face glowing.

Susan Harris bustled in and shooed the tall puncher out of the room. 'No more of that war talk, you two,' she scolded. 'Philly, yu've got to sleep. Lie down, now.'

'Hel—heck, I ain't tired, Miss Sue,' he complained. 'I just got through sleepin' a whole raft o' hours.'

'Now don't you argue with me, Mr. Philadelphia Sloane....' the girl was saying as Green left the room, leaving the boy grinning ruefully after him.

'Take about six months o' that to make him sick,' Green told his employer, who smiled fleetingly.

'Creates a few problems, though, Jim,' the older man said. 'I can't talk Susie into goin' into town, an' while she's here I'm not keen on goin' far from the house. Yet someone ought to ride over to tell the others that this Cameron's skulkin' around, in case anyone tries to take him on afore they know what they're gettin' into.'

'Yo're right,' Green agreed. 'I'll skedaddle over to Taylor's now. I can be there an' back in about two hours. I'll eat here, then ride over an' spread the word to the others.'

Without further ado he saddled up his horse and in a few more minutes was thundering westward towards the Lazy T.

* * *

Green had been gone about an hour when the sound of a wagon coming across the open plain brought Harris once more to the door, his hand shading his eyes as he scanned the prairie. He recognised the wagon immediately, and called in to his daughter reassuringly, 'It's Reb Johnstone's wagon—no need for alarm.'

A few minutes later the gangling Virginian was jumping down from the wagon seat, his cheerful Southern drawl bringing a smile to Harris's face. With him was his neighbour, Stan Newley, smiling nervously as always, and saying little. Harris rapidly decribed the events of the previous day, and the tall Southern's face was dark as he listened.

'He better not come snoopin' around mah place,' he said. 'I ain't afeared o' no damyankee gunman an' that's whatever.'

'Yu see him, yu stay away from him, Reb,' warned Harris. 'He's pizen mean an' he's fast enough with that gun to kill any of us afore we got rightly started.'

The Virginian's cheerful visage was serious as he listened to this warning.

'Mebbe yo're right at that, Jake,' he admitted. 'If'n Ah run into him, mebbe I'll pussyfoot some. Now: anything I c'n bring yu from Yavapai?'

'Yo're goin' into town?'

'Got to,' Newley said. 'Reb an' me got some fencin' to fix. We ordered some o' them reels o' fencin' wire from Kansas City, an' Lafferty's has got them down there.'

'Need some vittles, too,' Johnstone added. 'An' by cracky, I need me a good bottle o' sourmash. I'm plumb outa drinkin' likker.'

Harris shook his head. 'I hate to sound like a Jeremiah, Reb, but yu be sure an' tread lightly in town, hear? Nice an' easy, like. Any o' the Sabre boys down there, any sign o' this Cameron *hombre* an' yu just turn aroun' real quiet an' head for the Mesquites.'

'Hell, Jake, yu sound like an ol' woman,' complained Johnstone. 'We ain't lookin' for no fight.'

Harris nodded and turned to Newley. 'Stan, I'm puttin' it to yu. It's yore responsibility, yu hear me? Any sign o' trouble an' yu *git*. Okay?'

Newley blinked nervously and nodded. 'Don't ... don't yu worry, Jake. There'll be no trouble. We'll just pick up our stuff an' ...' As usual, his sentence ended unfinished.

Grumbling to himself about being 'treated like some half-wit infant', Reb Johnstone mounted his wagon. When Newley was aboard he swung the team around and cursed them up the trail into the pines at a hair-raising speed.

'Damn' fire-eatin' Rebel,' muttered Harris, shaking his head.

He stamped back into the house, where Susan, seeing his frown, asked, 'Do you think that man will be in Yavapai, Daddy?'

'I shore hope not,' said her father heavily. 'I shore as hell hope not.'

* * *

When Green reached the Lazy T he wasted no time in observing the social niceties but told the astonished Taylor about the events of the preceding day. Taylor wasted no more time than his visitor in confirming that he would take his men across to the Harris place immediately.

'There's nought here that would interest a manhunter, Jim,' he said. 'An' I've the feelin' that we'll all have a better chance together. I'll get my boys to ride over an' bring Kitson, Newley, an' Johnstone in to the JH as well. It'll be interestin' if our gun-totin' friend shows his face again.'

Green agreed to this arrangement gratefully; and Taylor agreed to explain to Harris that his rider had one more chore to do which would probably take him another twenty-four hours.

'Get on with whatever yu want to do, laddie,' Taylor told him. 'I'll tell Jake as soon as I get over there.'

The dour Scot's unexcited reaction to the bad news from Harris's place was a welcome tonic to Sudden, for he had been worried that Cameron's threats had shaken the old homesteader more than he cared to admit. With his friends beside him Jake would stand firm come hell or high water.

Sudden leaned forward and patted the glossy neck of his mount. 'Nig, we got some hard work ahead of us, an' yo're goin' to do most of it.' The horse nipped playfully at his hand as Sudden extended it, and he pulled the horse's ear, smiling. 'G'wan, yu walkin' gluepot, 'bout time yu worked for yore eats.' He pointed the black stallion's nose towards the northwest, where the frowning peaks of the Yavapai mountains towered against the sky.

Three-quarters of an hour later the sound of water echoing in a canyon reached his ears, and, spurring Nigger forward, the puncher came to a flat, open area. Ahead of him, like a giant crack in the earth's crust, was a canyon. Sudden dismounted and approached the edge. Down below, perhaps sixty or seventy feet, the waters of the Yavapai river boiled whitely over rapids.

'That'll be Apache Canyon,' he told himself. 'We go north.'

Mounting again, he followed the edge of the canyon northwards, noting that the ground here sloped sharply downwards. Soon the canyon was behind, and the river was a broad, flat stream which raced down from the mountains ahead. Trout leaped like flashes of rainbows out of the water, and once the cowboy caught a glimpse of a big bear lumbering through the brush. Off to the right was a spur of the range of high mountains ahead, lying like the paw of an animal across the foothills. Veering towards them, Sudden could see that the spur was scored by deep ravines on its western side; and he nodded to himself at this confirmation of his own thinking.

'Some o' them gullies will be deep enough to be used for pennin' cattle,' he soliloquised. 'My Gawd! but ain't they purty?'

This exclamation was elicited as the sun, slipping down in the west, touched the rims of the mountains with fire. The spur of hills which were the object of Green's attention turned bright ochre, brilliant orange, deep red, with dark black streaks where the gullies scored the rock.

'Purty or not, however, we got to take a gander at 'em a mite closer than this, Nig. Let's get at it.'

Responding to the light touch of his rider's heels, the black stallion lifted his heels and thundered towards their destination.

CHAPTER TWELVE

REB JOHNSTONE and Stan Newley got to Yavapai at about four o'clock, and the Virginian hitched his wagon team outside the general store. Stan Newley cocked an eye at the far-off mountains. The first dark mass of thunderheads that presaged one of the valley's sudden summer storms was piling up over the Yavapais.

'Better not stay too long, Reb,' he told his companion. 'Fixin' to storm some come nightfall.'

'All right, all right,' grinned Johnstone. 'Anythin' for a quiet life. Let's get them store goods.'

The two men spent the next hour and more choosing supplies for their homesteads, and loading the big, awkward spools of fencing wire into the bed of the wagon. A couple of bags of flour, some treacle, dried apples, a side of bacon, Arbuckle's coffee, some bags of chili beans. They covered the load with a tarpaulin; the wire spools were too bulky to cover properly.

'Hell with it,' Johnstone said. 'Lash 'em down. If they won't take a few drops o' rain on the way back they ain't goin' to be much use as fencin', are they?'

They lashed the tarp down, then stumped back into the store to settle their bill. When their business was completed Johnstone pounded his smaller companion on the back and said, 'Come on, Stan, an' I'll buy y'all that drink.'

Newly peered nervously down the street towards the lights of Tyler's saloon, already bold in the soft twilight easing its silent way into the valley. He squinted up at the Yavapais again.

'I'm worried about that storm, Reb,' he told the Southerner. 'If she rains afore we leave town we'll never get across Borracho with the wagon. We'll haveta detour all to hellangone around the edge o' the Badlands afore...'

'It won't rain afore we leave,' Johnstone told him. 'I got the word from one o' those rainmaker fellers on'y this mornin'.'

Newley hesitated still. 'Mebbe we oughta skip it, Reb.'

'Dang me if yu ain't wuss'n an ol' broody hen!' exploded the tall Virginian. 'Worry, worry, worry! Lissen: I'll tell yu what we-all goin' to do. We-all goin' to wander down to Tyler's, right? If we-all see any hosses at the rail belongin' to Sabre we turn aroun' an head straight home. If they's no Sabre nags we take our drink. Fair enough?'

Newley smiled for the first time, relief showing on his narrow face. 'Sounds fair,' he admitted. 'I just don't want no trouble.'

'Hell, Stan,' laughed Johnstone, 'yu oughta know by now it's allus the feller who says that who gets the most. Come on, cheer up! One li'l drink ain't goin' to hurt yu none!'

A quick inspection of the horses at the hitching-rail revealed that none of them bore the Sabre brand, although both men noticed a badly used bay standing, head down, and remarked on it.

Shaking their heads at the way some people treated good horse-flesh, the two homesteaders pushed into the saloon. The place was packed, with a heavy knot of people at the far end of the bar noisily celebrating, clustered around someone they couldn't see. Newley hesitated on the threshold, sensing the tense, brittle atmosphere of the place. A quick inspection of the room showed him no reason for this rising of his hackles and he shrugged and followed his friend into the bar. Johnstone called for drinks for both of them, and when Tyler had poured them said, 'Yu know whose that bay stallion outside is?'

The bartender cringed visibly, and an abrupt silence fell upon the entire saloon. Johnstone looked about him in amazement, unable to understand the reason for this cessation of all conversation, and unaware that his words had caused it.

As he stood, open mouthed, the knot of people at the end of the bar parted and a medium-sized, compactly built man pushed through the crowd towards him.

'Hoss is mine, mister,' said the man coldly. 'What of it?'

Johnstone, still nonplussed by the bated silence about him, regained a measure of his composure as he smiled down at the man in front of him. The man lounged easily against the bar, and there was no threat in his stance.

'Well, hell, mister ... meanin' no offence ... but he's shore in need o' rubbin' down. That's a mighty fine ani——'

The words froze on his lips as the man tossed a silver dollar on to the bar. It rang in the silence as it spun and slowly settled on the polished wood.

'There's a dollar,' the man sneered. 'Yu look like yu need it. Go out and rub the hoss down.'

Johnstone stood stock still for a moment, then took a step forward. As he did so, two things happened: he saw for the first time the cut-away holster low on the man's hip; and the saloon-owner, Tyler, laid a hand on his arm, blurting out, 'No, Reb! That's Wes Cameron!'

The Virginian stopped as if he had walked into a wall. Stan Newley, making sure that Cameron could see his hands plainly, touched his friend's arm.

'Come on, Reb. Reb—let's get out o' here,' he whispered.

Johnstone looked around uncertainly. He didn't want to back down from such a calculated insult, yet at the same time he was far from being so foolish as to think he could match this satanic killer.

'Ah ... Ah'm beggin' yore pardon, mister,' he mumbled, hating himself for saying the words. 'Ah shore didn't mean nothin' personal.'

Cameron did not deign to acknowledge the apology; the sneer on his face merely sharpened a fraction.

'What's yore name, Reb?' he grated.

'Name's Johnstone. Got a small place up in the Mesquites,' the big man stammered. 'Thisyere's m'neighbour, Stan Newley.'

'Yu men run big outfits? I'm needin' a job.'

'We only run small spreads, mister,' blurted Newley. 'We couldn't pay ... I mean we ain't got no need of ...' He fell silent as he realised the construction that might be placed upon his words by a man spoiling for trouble. Cameron shrugged. 'Pity. I'd admire working for a man who worries about horses the way Reb here does. I bet he thinks some animals is better than men, don't yu, Reb?'

With a flash of his old spirit Johnstone retorted. 'There's plenty o' men no better than animals.'

Cameron looked up at him sharply, and Johnstone fell back a pace. Once again Newley tugged at his sleeve, and he half turned to go. Cameron moved to place himself alongside Johnstone. 'Mebbe I'd better take a look at this hoss yo're so het up over,' he said.

The onlookers watched in silence as he shepherded the two men towards the door. Many of those watching would frankly not have been at all upset if a couple of the homesteaders were given a lesson in manners—at best they were only tolerated in Yavapai. Even if you didn't have anything good to say about Wes Cameron, they told each other, at least he was a cattleman.

As the trio pushed through the batwings there was a concerted rush for the windows. Wide-eyed, the patrons of Tyler's watched Cameron duck under the hitching-rail and start to look over his mount, allowing Stan Newley to half pull, half push his tall friend up the street towards where their wagon and team stood patiently awaiting their return. Newley clambered into the seat, and the Virginian took the bit of the lead horses in hand in order to swing them around on the street to point them north, where the first rumbles of thunder were threatening the rain-clouds over the mountains. As Johnstone swung the team out into the street the lights of the saloon fell upon him and the wagon with its half-covered load. It was at this moment that Cameron looked up, as if coincidentally, from his task.

'Yu! Nester!'

Cameron's voice cut the night like a north wind. The Virginian looked around, startled; Newley went rigid in the wagon seat. Behind Cameron, whom they could only just see against the bright blaze of the saloon's lights, the two men could see the entire patronage of Tyler's saloon awaiting their further discomfiture. Reb Johnstone's lips set in a thin line, and his back went straight.

'Reb, don't yu start nothin' now,' pleaded Newley. 'Please don't yu get into nothin', Reb!'

'Yu! Nester! What yu got in that wagon?'

Cameron's voice was flat and accusing.

'Wire.' Johnstone told him, equally flatly. He stood facing the gunman, his hand still holding the bit in the lead horse's mouth. His attitude was one of calm fearlessness.

'Wire? Yu stringin' wire in cattle country? By Gawd, where I come from yu'd be hung for that.'

'We ain't where yu come from,' Johnstone said tonelessly. 'Is that all yu wanted to know?'

'No,' Cameron said evilly. 'There's one more thing. How come a man who strings wire in cattle country has got the nerve to tell a cattleman how to take care o' his hoss?'

Johnstone shrugged.

'Cameron, Ah know who yu are an' Ah know what yore reputation is. Yu ain't goin' to prod me into no gunfight. If yu've said yore piece Ah'm about ready to leave.'

Cameron nodded. His voice was soft and hardly carried as far as Johnstone; most of those inside the saloon did not hear it at all, so quietly were the words spoken. But Johnstone heard them. Cameron said, 'No wonder yu ——'s lost the war.' With a muted curse the big Southerner dropped his hand from the bit and pawed for the gun at his side. Cameron did not move until Reb's hand had closed on the butt, lifted the gun clear, and cocked it. Before Reb could complete the last part of his draw, and bring the gun level to fire, Cameron made his play. Nobody watching saw his hand move, but there was his gun belching fire: once, twice, three times. Reb Johnstone was hurled backwards against the horses by the force of the bullets, and the horses shied violently. They reared upwards and away from the sound of the shots, throwing the half-paralysed Newley into the street. Johnstone half rose on his elbow as Newley scrabbled towards him on hands and knees while the wagon and team thundered down the street. Unthinkingly Newley reached towards his hip pocket for a bandanna with which to staunch the great gouts of blood staining his friend's chest, and in a cold, clear split second realised as he did so what he had done.

'Don't touch it!' he heard Cameron yell, and then he heard the shot that hammered him backwards. His last thought was that he had given the gunman a permit to shoot him and the last word he uttered was 'stupid'.

Cameron stood by the hitching-rail, his body tense, half-crouched; the two bodies lay still and silent in the dust. Tom Appleby came racing up the street, gun in hand. He slid to a stop as Cameron wheeled around, the light glinting on the ready gun, and for a cold instant the lawman braced himself against the shock of a shot as the thought touched his mind: 'He's killin' mad!' Then the light behind Cameron's eyes died, and he straightened slowly, holstering his gun. A cold smile played about his mouth.

'Pure self-defence, Marshal. There's about sixty people here saw the whole thing. The tall one went for his gun first. When I downed him the other one tried to draw on me.' He waved a hand at the still-silent watchers, a few of whom were edging out into the street for a closer look at the scene of the killing. 'I'm bettin' all these folks'll tell yu it was self-defencc,' Cameron repeated.

'I'm aimin' to ask every one o' them,' Appleby told him. 'If it was self-defence yo're clear. But don't think o' leavin' town for a few days.'

Cameron grinned with evil enjoyment. 'Why, Marshal, yu know I wouldn't dream o' disobeyin' yu.'

Appleby stood for a moment regarding Cameron. He knew that the witnesses would swear it was self-defence: Cameron had bought enough drinks to ensure sympathy, and he had no doubt that Johnstone and Newley had made the first move. Cameron would have seen to that. A wave of disgust touched his face for a moment, and then he turned away to get help in moving the bodies off the street. As the crowd returned to the saloon the first real thunder rolled down from the Yavapais like a rock slide and the sticky rain started to fall.

CHAPTER THIRTEEN

As Sudden pulled Nigger to a stop at the crest of yet another rise he realised that the big stallion was tired. He knew that the black would go on until his big heart gave out, but to push him too hard would not only be cruel but downright foolhardy.

'Man on foot'd last about a day at most in these parts,' he muttered. 'Shore is cold.'

He had been investigating each of the canyons that lay in the spur of the mountains, so far without any indication at all that there were any other forms of life up here at all except wild animals. The ground was hard and bare; even if a large herd had been driven across it there would have been only the faintest of tracks.

'Shore looks like a wild-goose chase, Nig,' he told the horse, and then, with an eye scanning the lowering cloud over the peaks to the west, 'an' if we ain't under cover afore long we're goin' to sleep wet tonight.'

The big horse brought his head up sharply as thunder crashed among the peaks. There was a misty, damp feeling in the air that struck to the rider's bones.

'If this is mountain livin', give me the desert every time,' he shivered. 'Come on, boy. One more, an' then we'll bed down for the night.'

The light was becoming increasingly bad as he headed the horse down the slope and along the floor of yet another of the arroyos. This one looked no different to the many others he had already investigated. The peaks towered ahead, shrouded in grey mist. Once or twice lightning flickered, lighting the mist with sinister colours. On both sides of the rider high hills rose sharply, their outlines vague. He peered ahead disconsolately.

'Don't look any better than the others,' he told himself. Just as he did so, however, a dark shape loomed on his right, then lumbered off into the brush.

The puncher sat erect in the saddle, all traces of weariness disappearing. A broad grin appeared on his face, and he patted the horse, whose ears had perked up in interest.

'Yu seen him too, did yu?' Sudden smiled. 'Best lookin' cow I seen in many a long day, Nig. Let's take a look-see if he's got any friends.'

Nigger was a trained cow-pony. It took no more than a touch of his rider's heels to send him leaping forward after the retreating steer and, within moments, Sudden found himself amid a milling bunch of perhaps thirty or forty cattle.

A quick glance showed him that they carried the Sabre brand, and his lips pursed thoughtfully. Pulling his horse's head around, Sudden headed on up the darkening canyon. The building thunderstorm was casting its pall over the entire area; he could no longer see the mouth of the canyon. Overhead, thunder rolled more regularly.

'Fixin' to storm,' Sudden told himself. 'I wonder if there's some kind o' shelter up here?'

As if in answer to his unspoken question a light sprang into view as he rounded a slight bend in the canyon. He kicked Nigger into a canter, and in a moment could see the outline of a small cabin hulking against the canyon wall. He rode openly towards it, and when he was within a few yards of the house yelled, 'Hello, the house!'

The door opened, and a bent old figure appeared, peering into the near-darkness.

'Who's there?' demanded a crotchety voice. 'Who's there?'

Without answering, Sudden dismounted and led the horse forward. The light in the cabin gave him the advantage, for he could now plainly see that the occupant was an old man, whose greying hair and silvered beard glinted in the lamplight.

'It's me—Green,' the cowboy called. 'Where can I put the horse?'

'Tether him in back o' the cabin,' called the old man, 'an' come in so I can shut this danged door!'

After he had done as he was bid, Sudden went around the house and opened the door. The old man was pottering over a battered old iron stove, and the delicious smell of fresh coffee was strong in the room.

'Coffee smells good,' Green observed.

'It's fair,' was the oldster's comment. 'I had enough practice.'

The puncher's eye travelled swiftly over the tiny cabin. It was barely furnished; in one corner were two bunks, one above the other. A table, some chairs, a few rude shelves, and the pot-bellied iron stove were all its furnishings. The only window was boarded up, and the floor was beaten earth, stamped flat by years of use.

The old man was about seventy, Sudden guessed, and if his hands were any indication he had spent many years of his life in manual labour. Sudden risked a guess.

'Had any luck with yore pannin'?' he asked.

The old man turned, raising his eyebrows. 'How'd yu—oh, I suppose Jim told yu. Nope, not much.'

'Yu reckon yu'll find somethin' up in these mountains?' Sudden continued, playing along with the conversation which, from the old man's first remark, might lead to something.

'Got to be,' the old man said, pouring steaming mugs of coffee for them both. 'Got to be. I feel it in my bones. Come on, boy, set yoreself down. What yu say yore name was—Green?'

'That's it,' Sudden replied. 'Jim sets a mite easier.'

'Jim. Yu both got the same name. Must be confusin' at times.'

Determined to play this string out until it led somewhere, Sudden said, 'Ain't as many times a day as yu'd think. I'm out on the range mostly....'

The old man nodded. 'Used to know a feller named Green in Amarillo. Tom Green. Any relation o' yourn?' His old eyes were bright and shrewd in the lamplight over the rim of his coffee cup. Sudden shook his head.

'I'm from New Mexico,' he told the old man. 'This is good coffee.'

The oldster was not to be diverted from his interest as easily as that. 'I ain't seen yu afore,' he said. 'How come Jim sends yu up here instead o' Mado?'

'Mado's a mite off colour,' Green lied. 'Yu ain't the on'y problem Jim's got.'

The man's words had confirmed his suspicions; this canyon was a hideout for stolen Sabre beef, and Dancy was behind their theft. It was now necessary to discover whether this old man knew of that; if he did, Sudden knew that he was far from being out of danger. The old man nodded at his remark about Dancy.

'S'pose yo're right. Sabre's a big spread. Jim often sez to me, "Shorty," he sez, "you think yoreself lucky yu ain't got my troubles." He grinned toothlessly. "All yu do is set here an' mind cows for me," he sez. "Yu get yore money an' yu got no ambitions, 'ceptin' to find a paylode in these hills." He's a great josher, that Jim.'

'He shore is,' grinned Sudden, finding himself liking this unpretentious old man. But he had to know the truth. 'Jim tol' me to tell yu he was goin' to ride up here an' drive these cattle clear to the Army reservation an' sell 'em. Said to tell yu he'd split fifty-fifty, an' yu could both retire.'

He watched the old man narrowly as he spoke these words, but Shorty wheezed with laughter, slapping his thigh so hard that dust flew from his ancient corduroys. 'That Dancy,' he coughed, 'he shore is a josher!' There was absolutely no nuance in his voice, and Sudden was convinced that the old man had no real knowledge of Dancy's intentions. For some reason he found himself very glad.

'Yu been in these parts long, Shorty?' he asked.

'Twenty years, man an' boy,' the old man said proudly. 'I was here when Lafe Gunnison first come to these parts.'

'Yu know Gunnison?'

'Shore I know him. He wouldn't know me, but I know him. Know his boy, Randy, too. He was up here a while back.'

It was Sudden's turn to look surprised, and the old man noticed his reaction.

'That surprise yu, does it?' he cackled. 'Surprised me, too! I allus thought Randy was as much use as a fifth wheel on a wagon, but he rode up here with Dancy all the same.'

'What did he come for?' asked Green. 'I thought Dancy handled all the day-to-day chores?'

'Yo're danged right,' said the old man. 'Told Randy as much. He told me to shet my mouth, mind my own business. Figgered. Allus had a mean mouth, Randy. Anyways, him an' Dancy was here a coupla hours, then they rode off north. Expect they was headin' for Riverton.'

Sudden nodded. The revelation that Randolph Gunnison was a party to the theft of the Sabre's cattle was astounding. Could it be that Dancy had razzle-dazzled the rancher's son? He asked a question of the old man.

'Friendly? I should smile, they was! Thicker'n flies in

a Pawnee camp, those two. More coffee?'

Green held out his cup silently. The involvement of Randolph Gunnison in the thefts now put an entirely different light on his own theories about the troubles in the Yavapai.

'Randy went to some fancy school back east, didn't he?' he asked Shorty.

'Fancy school, yep. Back east, nope,' said the old prospector, succinctly. 'He went to some place in Santy Fé. That's a year or two ago, mind.'

'Shore, I know that,' Green agreed. 'He never did spend overmuch time on the Sabre, far as I can gather.'

'Never more than he had to,' agreed Shorty. 'Randy likes cards, gals, an' likker. It's work he can't stand, or so they says.'

Outside the cabin the storm broke. Green heard the rain spattering like shot on the tin roof of the shack, and he rose to his feet.

'I better 'tend to my hoss,' he told the old man. Shorty nodded, and the puncher let himself into the driving storm. The rain was coming down now like a solid sheet of water, and lightning flickered over the far peaks, the thunder booming in its wake. Sudden led Nigger across the open space behind the house to a lean-to on the far side of the corral there. Unsaddling the stallion, he rubbed the horse down, telling him. 'It ain't the Palace Ho-tel, Nig, but yu been in wuss.'

Slapping the glossy haunch, he donned the slicker he had unstrapped from the saddle roll and sloshed his way back through the mud to the cabin, his mind busy with the facts which Shorty had unwittingly revealed.

He opened the door and found himself facing the unwavering muzzle of an old Dragoon Colt; holding it fully cocked was the old man, who was smiling like a cat at a mouse-hole.

'What's this about?' asked Green mildly.

'Yu ain't no Sabre rider!' snapped Shorty. 'H'ist yore paws, mister, an' start explainin' yoreself!'

Green grinned, his smile disconcerting the old man.

'Ease off on that hammer, ol' timer,' the cowboy said. 'Yu might just blow a hole in me afore I got time to reply.'

'I might jest blow a hole in yu for the hell of it,' retorted Shorty. 'An' I won't tell yu again! Reach!'

Green raised his arms obligingly, and as he did so, the front of the enveloping slicker rose with them. In that same swift movement the cape caught the menacing barrel of the cap and ball pistol, knocking it upwards. The old man pulled the trigger by reflex, and the shot boomed harmlessly into the ceiling. Before Shorty could recover himself Sudden had seized the revolver and twisted it from the old man's grasp.

Shorty reeled backwards and then surged forward again, trying ineffectually to land a blow on the tall puncher's body. Green held the old man off with some difficulty; eventually he exerted his whipcord strength and frogmarched the oldster to a chair, where Shorty sat, winded and cursing weakly.

'Now rest easy a moment,' Sudden told him. 'Yo're due an explanation, an' I'll give it to yu. First, I'm a-puttin' yu on yore word yu won't try nothin'. Agreed?'

Shorty glared at him defiantly for a moment, and then shrugged. 'If yo're aimin' to steal them cattle, mister, yo're loony. The Sabre'll track yu down an' skin yu for a saddle-blanket.'

'Yo're probably right,' Green smiled. 'Exceptin' that the Sabre don't know these cattle is up here.'

The old man snorted. 'Yo're loco, Green—if that's yore name!'

Sudden shook his head, and in level tones told the old prospector what had brought him up into the Yavapais, and of his suspicions that the thefts of Sabre beef had been engineered to throw suspicion upon the homesteaders. The involvement of Dancy and Randolph Gunnison was plain, but he was unable to pin down the reason for their actions—yet. All this and more he told the old prospector, who sat and listened with first disbelief, then astonishment, and in the end with exclamations of disgust and anger.

'To think them thievin' mangy coyotes roped me in on their dirty dealin's,' he raged. 'If Lafe Gunnison'd run on to this canyon he'd a' hung me higher'n Haman! An' I wouldn't've stood a chance.'

Green nodded. 'Dancy an' Randy Gunnison could've

easy called yu a liar if yu'd got the chance to name them. The old man'd never believe his son was stealin' Sabre beef.'

The old man let loose another round of imaginative cursing, and then asked, 'Where do yu fit into all this, Jim?'

'That's easy answered,' Sudden told him. 'I work for Jake Harris over in the Mesquites.'

'Them homestead outfits, yu mean?' the old man asked. When Green nodded affirmatively, Shorty mused, 'I ain't never met any o' them, but if yo're with 'em I'll stake my washin's they're honest. Yu reckon Dancy an' Randy been sellin' Sabre beef to these *hombres* in Riverton?'

Green nodded. 'It's got to be that way, Shorty,' he told the prospector. 'I still don't quite see what's behind it, though. If Dancy steals Sabre beef an' sells it that's easy to figger: he needs money.'

'Mebbe Randy Gunnison needs money, too,' suggested Shorty. 'He shore gambles heavy.'

'Could be,' admitted Green. 'But I figger his old man'd bail him out. Anyway, puttin' the blame on the homesteaders could on'y lead to big trouble. It looks like Dancy an' Gunnison was aimin' to start range war trouble here, an' get them nesters off the land they're on. But why?'

The old man shook his head. 'Beats me, Jim. I can tell yu one thing: they ain't no gold nor silver in them hills. I been over ever' foot o' them. Not a smidgin' anyplace.'

They talked for a long while in the flickering lamplight. The old man started reminiscing about the old days in this territory, when a lone white man was easy prey for the Apaches who roamed the hills. He had come out searching for gold or silver as a young man, fallen in love with the country, and stayed.

'Them bucks near took my hair one time or two,' he told Sudden, 'but I allus foxed 'em. Figgered I'd find that pot o' gold one day. Reckon I will yet. She's up in these mountains someplace.'

Green smiled. He knew the type well. This old desert-rat would roam the mountains until the day he died, seeking the precious yellow metal. Green had seen many like him—he recalled his adventures in Deadwood,* when thousands upon thousands of prospectors had invaded the Black Hills looking for riches. He remembered the old man who had told him that: 'It ain't the gold, boy, it's findin' it that's important. Yu can't know what it's like, findin' a vein, stickin' yore pick into a solid lump o' money...' Shorty was ill: the gold-sickness was one of which very few men were cured. But he knew that the old timer would no more change his existence than he would fly.

Shorty was talking on, about the wild days in Arizona, when it had been a haven for every outlaw north of the border.

'They all come through these parts,' he told Sudden. 'Billy the Kid, the James boys. They'd head for Mexico until the Law gave up on lookin' for them, an' then they'd head back an' start up ag'in.' Shorty shook his head. 'They was great times,' he said.

They talked into the night, with Sudden listening with real interest to the tales the old man—a born story-teller—recounted. Hangings, stampedes, gunfights, gold rushes—Shorty had seen them all.

'They ever have any trouble in these parts afore recent times?' he asked the old man.

Shorty shook his head. 'Naw,' he said. 'Ain't been any real trouble in Yavapai valley since the Jefferson boys was caught, up in the Mesquites, an' shot it out with a posse.'

Green looked his interest, and the old man continued. 'It was back in '65—no, '66,' he said. 'Them Jefferson boys was skallyhootin' around robbin' stagecoaches an' the odd bank. Law got word they was down in the Mesquites an' treed the whole passel o' them. Killed 'em all but two, an' they hanged Jack Jefferson an' his kid brother after they was took back to Yuma an' tried.'

'But the troubles at Sabre on'y started recently?' the puncher prompted.

'Fur as I know,' Shorty said. 'I ain't stuck my nose in any further'n necessary. I stayed up here an' looked after the cows. Now an' again I'd ask Dancy or Mado what was happenin', but they'd tell me to mind my own concerns,

* Related in *Sudden—Goldseeker* (Corgi Books).

an' I reckoned to do just that.'

They sat a while in silence, and then the old man rose. 'I'm right tired from all this reminiscin',' he told the younger man. 'If it's all the same to yu, I'm turnin' in. An' Jim——' he turned to face Sudden squarely. 'I'm thankin' yu for settin' me straight. I'm quittin' this place in the mornin', shore.'

Green looked the old man straight in the eyes. 'That's a wise move, Shorty,' he said. 'I got an idea yu could be my ace-in-the-hole. I reckon yu better come back to the Harris place with me, an' stay out o' sight until the right time. That sound sensible to yu?'

''Bout the most sensible thing I've heard in a while,' the old man grinned. 'I'm obliged, Jim. Yu can rely on me.'

The puncher smiled. 'Knew it all along,' he told Shorty.

Presently, the old man's snores reverberated in the tiny cabin. Sudden still sat, his feet on the table, his eyes fixed unseeingly upon the dull glow of the stove. The frown of concentration was deep between his eyebrows, and his thoughts were of treachery and greed.

CHAPTER FOURTEEN

'GUNNISON! God damn his black heart!' The words were roared rather than spoken, and the man who uttered them was Jacob Harris. 'The thievin' polecat hired that gunman as shore as Gawd made little apples!'

Tom Appleby, who had brought the news of the killing of Reb Johnstone and Stan Newley to the homesteader, opened his mouth to say something. Before he could speak, the old man continued in the same vein:

'We know he hired that dawg Cameron! Yu know it, an' I know it, Tom, an' we're helpless, we can't touch him. Two good men under the ground, an' the killer walks around Yavapai as free as air! I've got a good mind——'

'If yo're goin' to say what I think yo're goin' to say, yo're about to prove yu ain't,' snapped Appleby. 'Jake, I'm as sorry as yu are about those men, but goin' to Yavapai an' startin' a battle in town ain't goin' to bring them back!'

The old man banged his fist on the table, setting crockery to rattling on the shelves.

'I ain't goin' to set here an' do nothin'!' he bellowed.

'Yes—yu—are!' gritted Appleby. 'Jake, I'm warnin' yu—don't come into town, an' don't even think about it! If what yu say is true—an' I, for one, ain't shore Gunnison is behind this Cameron feller—then yu'll be playin' into his hands by tryin' to take on Cameron. He's a cold killer, Jake. Yu wouldn't stand a chance an' yu know it!'

'Tom, I guess yo're right,' admitted Harris wearily. 'Tho' it goes ag'in my nature to say it. I want to thank yu for ridin' up an' lettin' me know.'

'Tom, ye'll let us send someone in for the bodies?' put in Alex Taylor.

Appleby pursed his lips, as though weighing the advisability of Taylor's suggestion. Then he nodded. 'Yu send in one o' yore hired men,' he told them. 'Mebbe yu can spare yore Swede, Terry?'

Kitson nodded. 'Shore,' he agreed.

The three homesteaders were still stunned by the news that the Marshal had brought. Subsequent to Green's visit, Taylor had arrived at the JH, and Kitson had been sent for. They had watched on tenterhooks for the possible return of the gunman, and, as the night progressed, had become more and more perturbed about the two men who had gone into town. Appleby's arrival had sent them to their posts by the windows, guns ready; Cameron would not find them again unprepared, they had vowed. The single horseman had been covered every inch of the way until he had been identified as the town Marshal. Appleby had been brief and blunt. He told them of the events in Yavapai, and of the fact that there were plenty of witnesses to the gunman's claim that he had killed in self-defence.

Now Kitson, Taylor, and Jake Harris sat glumly at the big table, their faces drawn.

Appleby, uncomfortable in the silence, broke it with a question:

'What will happen to Johnstone an' Newley's places?'

Jake Harris looked at him glumly, uncomprehending.

'Yu aim to file on the land, Jake?' Appleby persisted.

Harris shrugged. 'T'ain't likely,' he told the lawman. 'I can't use the extra acres without help.'

Appleby looked around. 'That reminds me,' he said lightly. 'I ain't seen yore man Green. Where's he at?'

'He's out on the range,' Harris said quickly. Alex Taylor glanced at him, but kept his counsel, although Appleby did not miss the significant puzzlement in the Scot's eyes. 'He oughta be back afore long,' Harris told the Marshal, and Appleby nodded, more or less satisfied by this.

'Jake, I wish I could say how sorry I am,' he began.

Harris waved the words aside. 'Yu done all yu could, an' I'm thankin' yu, Tom. I just plain don't know what to do. We ain't equipped for this kind o' fightin'. If it was out in the open we'd fight—an' gladly! But seein' yore neighbours cut down, knowin' they had no more chance than if they'd been bushwhacked ... it takes the heart out of a man.' He rose heavily; the others watched him gloomily. 'Yu'll stay an' take a bite?' he asked the Marshal.

'Thank yu, Jake, I'll do that.'

'Susie'll fix yu somethin'. She's tendin' the boy.'

Appleby looked his interest. 'How's he doin'?'

'He'll be fine. Soon be able to hobble around, I guess. Tom, yu go on into the kitchen, tell Susie to give yu some cawfee.'

He walked over to the window and looked out blindly, chewing on his old pipe, while Kitson and Taylor stirred uncomfortably. Appleby nodded to them and went through into the kitchen, where Susan was busily stirring something which smelled deliciously in an iron pot. She turned at his footsteps, her pretty face flushed from the heat.

'Oh, Tom,' she exclaimed. 'You'll be in need of some "cawfee", I should think. Could you manage a piece of fresh-baked pie with it?' A dimple showed in her cheek as she smiled.

'Reckon I could force one down,' he told her.
'Coming up,' she said. 'Sit down at the table.'

He watched her as she bustled about the little kitchen, and his eyes travelled over her, weighing the supple slimness of her waist, her rounded form, the youthful spring of her walk. Conscious of his scrutiny Susan turned to face him, a slow flush mounting beneath her skin. To conceal her embarrassment she asked him whether the man, Cameron, was still in Yavapai.

'Shore is,' Appleby told her. 'I can't move him on without a reason.'

'I'd move him on if I were Marshal!' she exclaimed vehemently.

'Yu got to admit, yore viewpoint'd be a mite biased,' he told her in a reasonable tone. 'Susie, yu know my job is keepin' the peace. That means for everybody, not just for one bunch o' folks yu happen to prefer. If it was just me, I'd do her—just to make yu smile.'

'Why Tom Appleby,' she said mockingly, 'I do believe you're flirting with me!'

'Might be at that,' he said, attacking the apple-pie she set before him with gusto. When he had finished he leaned back with a sigh and reached for the makin's. 'Girl,' he told her, 'yo're a miracle in these parts.'

'Tom, you're staring at me in such a funny way...' she said.

'Am, now yu mention it,' he said unperturbed.

'Well, stop, it makes me uncomfortable,' she ordered.

'Don't aim to stop,' he said, rising to his feet and laying the unfinished cigarette alongside his plate. 'Susie, I wanted yu the first time I seen yu. Won't yu think about bein' my wife?'

Susan stopped in the middle of the room, her mouth a wide 'o' of astonishment. 'Why, Tom ... oh, now stop that teasing!' she said, thinking he was joking.

He crossed the kitchen and stood before her, and put his hands upon her shoulders. 'I mean every word I say, girl.' His voice was husky. 'I'm not rich, but one o' these days...' He hesitated for a moment, then went on, 'Well, I'd see yu never wanted. Clothes, a big house, travel—all yu'd ever want, girl! Won't yu think about it?'

Susan was nonplussed by his directness, and as she

studied him from beneath lowered eyelashes she admitted to herself that probably many women would find Tom Appleby an attractive man. And yet...

'I'm very fond of you, Tom...' she began.

'But yu don't love me.' He snapped his fingers. 'That for love! Girl, I'd make yu care for me.'

Despite herself Susan found her pulses pounding. But behind the Marshal's eyes she divined for the first time the egotism and the ambition that lurked there, and they repelled her. His hands clamped upon her shoulders as she tried to move back. Unconsciously she began to struggle against his grip, but he was relentless. His arms encircled her, and powerless in his grasp she found herself being lifted towards him. His head bent, his thin lips pressed towards her own and a small shrill note of panic sounded in the girl's mind. Suddenly his grip relaxed and she collapsed, half swooning, in a chair as a familiar voice rasped, 'Stand back an' stand still, Marshal!'

Half turning, Susan saw the tall, saturnine James Green, who had come into the room unnoticed by either of them. A pistol pointed unwaveringly at Appleby, and the puncher's eyes were like shifting ice under a glacier.

'Looks like I got back at just the right time,' he gritted. 'Yu all right, ma'am?'

'Yes, Jim ... it's all right. Just ... a ... misunderstanding.'

Appleby faced Sudden's drawn gun unafraid; his face was dark with anger.

'Green, yo're interferin' in somethin' that don't concern yu!' he warned the puncher. 'I just asked Susan to be my wife.'

'Looked to me like she turned yu down,' was the cold reply.

'Don't push yore luck too far, Green,' said Appleby, an edge on his voice.

Sudden grinned icily. 'How far would yu say too far was, Marshal?' Turning to the girl, who had now recovered from her ordeal and was watching the two men uncertainly, he added, 'Say the word, ma'am, an' I'll toss this coyote out on his ear.'

Susan Harris laid a hand on his forearm.

'No, Jim. It was a ... misunderstanding. Truly. I think Tom made a mistake.'

'He better not make it again,' rapped the puncher.

Appleby made a good effort of pretending not to hear Sudden's words. He turned to Susan Harris. 'I won't give up, Susan. I meant every word I said.'

'I hope that is not true,' she said gravely, and turned away.

'I meant every word *I* said, too, Marshal,' interrupted Green, as the lawman took a step forward. 'Yu better have a damn good reason for showin' yore face in these parts again!'

The Marshal wheeled about, a snarl disfiguring his handsome face. 'I won't forget this!' he threatened. Gone was the friendly smile; in its place was the expression of a killer wolf.

If it frightened Sudden he gave no indication of it, but said, 'Yu better not! Fade!'

Appleby turned on his heel without a word and rushed out of the house, his face like thunder. The men inside watched him go in astonishment, turning towards Sudden, who brought Susan in from the kitchen with him. As Appleby's horse thundered off up the trail he told them with a smile, 'Miss Susan just turned down the Marshal's marriage offer. He's so peeved about it I'd misdoubt he'll be around for a while.' He shook his head when they bombarded him with further questions, and taking the girl by the arm, he led her back into the kitchen.

'Yu look like yu need yore mind takin' off yore own troubles,' he told her. A faint smile broke through her troubled expression and Sudden smiled in response. 'I brung an ol' pack-rat back here with me who ain't et nothin' but beans an' bacon for so long he's plain slaverin' at the smells comin' out o' this kitchen. Ol' Doc Green's goin' to prescribe a course o' feedin' an' fattenin' for him, an' a course o' lookin' after lost sheep for yu. By the way, how's yore patient?'

With a startled 'Oh!' Susan remembered her charge in the small bedroom, and ran eagerly towards it.

'Looks like he's no worse,' Sudden told himself, with a smile. Then his expression hardened as he looked through the window to where the faint haze of dust raised by Appleby's horse still sparkled brightly in the sunlight.

CHAPTER FIFTEEN

LAFE GUNNISON was in a foul mood. Dancy, who had seen the storm brewing, had wisely found something requiring his attention elsewhere. The rest of the hands were out about their daily chores. The cook, who poked his head around the door to find out if the boss wanted any more coffee, was stampeded back to his kitchen by a blistering round of invective.

'Dang me if workin' here don't git more like bein' in the Army every day,' muttered that worthy. 'If yu don't do it yu gets chewed out, an' when yu offer to do it yu gets chewed out. Dang me if the Army ain't better, come to think of it!' Continuing his complaints under his breath, the panhandler rattled angrily amid his cluttered pots and pans.

The old man inside did not hear him, any more than he watched the clouds drifting across the cerulean sky through the grimy windows of the ranchhouse. His mind was circling like a fox in a foot-trap, trying to pin down some small thing that he had heard, somewhere, some hint that remained in his mind and gnawed away, spoiling his sleep, his digestion, and his peace of mind.

Silently he catalogued his worries: the constant loss of cattle reported by Dancy, and Randy's continued harping upon them, and his insistence that the homesteaders would eventually steal the Sabre from under his, Lafe Gunnison's, nose, while he sat and vacillated. Against this he had to set the visit of the cool-talking cowboy from the Mesquites, who had so contemptuously dismissed the danger inherent in riding on to Sabre land, and who had claimed that the attempted assassination of Susan Harris and the boy—what was it he called himself? Philadelphia—might have been carried out by someone on Sabre. Gunnison felt now as he had felt when he first talked to the man called Green. Something told him, assured him, convinced him, that Green was more than just another drifting cowboy and anything but a liar. And that boy . . . the amazing resemblance had shaken him more than he cared to admit. While every fibre of him cried out to believe, he denied himself the luxury of sentimentality. It was coincidence, no more. Impossible! His mind was still revolving around the same thoughts when his son came into the room and sprawled into a chair near the window. Lafe Gunnison eyed his offspring with distaste.

'Decided to honour us with yore presence again, eh?' he growled. 'When I was yore age I was chousing cows at daybreak, 'stead o' lollin' in bed until mid-mornin'.'

'Father, please don't start all that again,' Randy protested. 'My head's aching.'

'If yu can't handle yore likker, stay away from Tyler's,' growled the old man. He rumbled on about Randy's constant habit of leaving without saying where he was going, staying away without giving anyone any notion of when he would be back. . . . Randy Gunnison sat and listened sullenly to the tirade. His father was a dull old fool, Randy felt, who had nothing in his head except cattle. There was plenty of money, but his father could think of nothing to do with it except spend it on more improvements to Sabre. Even the yearly trips to St. Louis or Phoenix were long, boring rounds of whisky-drinking with other cattlemen, buyers, drovers, full of dreary reminiscences about tawdry cattle towns and long-dead companions.

'The sooner the old fool dies the better,' Randy thought viciously. But he knew his father was as tough as rawhide; it would be years. Randy Gunnison sat wishing for some act of providence, some accident to strike the old man down. 'If I had the ranch,' he thought, 'it would change things!' As he thought it, however, a cold sense of dread closed in on him and he imagined what this hugely powerful man who was his father might do if he had any inkling of the things in which his son was involved. At least, Randy told himself, it was going to mean money now, instead of in ten or twenty years time when the old fool cashed in his checks.

'He'll never die,' Randy whispered to himself. 'Never.' In his half-hearing, the diatribe continued as Lafe Gunnison paced the floor. Same old story, Randy thought wearily, I've heard it so many times ... maybe it was because I never had a mother ... how much he wished she'd left Hank and taken Randy instead ... how hard he had worked to make something of himself ... started off as a thirty a month cowboy and built this ranch from nothing with these hands .... Randy turned off his hearing again as his father ranted on. With some difficulty he recalled what had started this off, and then remembered that he had some news which would at least stem the avalanche of words.

'If you'll let me speak,' he told his father coldly, 'I'll tell you some news which will make you very glad I went to Yavapai.'

'Yu waster, what could yu tell me to make me glad except the news yu'd had yore head changed?'

'Father, stop yelling and listen to me. Two men were killed in Yavapai yesterday. Their names were Johnstone and Newley. Aren't you interested?'

The old man had stopped in mid-stride, thunderstruck.

'What's that yu say? Killed? Who killed them? Who?' He crossed the room in two strides and stood towering over his son. 'If yu had anythin' to do with it ...'

'Oh, don't be so stupid, Father!' snapped the younger man. 'If you'll be quiet for a minute I'll tell you. Shouting at the top of your voice isn't going to help.'

The old man nodded, swallowed deeply, and retreated. He sat down heavily on the arm of an old chair.

'Go ahead,' he ordered.

Randy Gunnison proceeded to describe the events of the preceding day in vivid detail, relishing the look on his father's face. He described how the two homesteaders had come into the saloon in Yavapai, their mild quarrel with the gunman Cameron, and the violent events which had ensued in the street. He omitted only that he had seen the whole affair from the vantage point of a bedroom window over Tyler's, in a room occupied by one of the girls employed there. A faint sneer crossed Randy's face. Maybe I ought to tell him just to see what he'd do, he thought. The old fool'd probably have a stroke. With an effort he put these thoughts aside and paid attention to the question his father was repeating, impatiently this time.

'I asked yu—is his name Wes Cameron?' When Randy indicated that this was so, the old man asked, 'How long has he been in town?'

'I don't know. A day or two. Not long.'

'Appleby allowin' a killer like that to stay in town ain't my idea o' good town-Marshallin',' growled Gunnison.

'I heard they had a run-in of sorts,' Randy said. 'Appleby agreed to some kind of truce as long as Cameron didn't get involved in any trouble. He braced Cameron after the fight and Cameron backed him down.'

'Tom Appleby backed down?' The old man frowned. 'That ain't like him.'

'It was a clear case of self-defence. There were dozens of witnesses. Nothing Tom could have done.'

'So he's still in town?'

'Cameron? Yes, and I can't see anyone making him leave until he's good and ready. The man's a born killer.'

'Nobody's a born killer, boy,' the old man told him. 'Yu got to learn it.'

Randy remembered what he had been told to say.

'There was some talk that Harris might be behind it.'

Lafe Gunnison looked as if his son had just offered to sell him the moon.

'Yu must be plumb loco!' he grated. 'Whyfor would Harris hire his neighbours killed?'

'I'm sure I don't know,' said Randy cunningly, 'unless he was trying to get control of their land for some reason.'

'I can't see it, just the same,' the rancher said.

'Well ... who gets the land? Answer me that!' snapped Randy.

'It ain't logical...' Gunnison began, but his son did not allow him to continue his sentence.

'No, not to you,' sneered Randy. 'You'll wait until it's

too late, hoping that in the end they'll turn out to be decent fellows and live and let live. If Harris gets control of all that land up there you'll never shift him off it! And if you think we're losing stock now you wait until he's got a hard-case crew up there. This Cameron, that other one, Green, they're the same breed.'

Old Lafe Gunnison looked at his son with a strange light coming into his eyes.

'Yu don't think much o' me, do yu, boy?'

'My dear father, what has that got to do with what we're discussing?'

'Let me ask yu a question, Randy.' There was an intent gleam in Lafe Gunnison's eyes. He rose from the chair and stood tall, facing his sprawling son. 'Whyfor're yu so keen to make me get into a fight with Jake Harris?'

Randy stood up and faced his father.

'Because if you don't, then one of these days he'll bring a fight here and that will be the end of Sabre!'

Lafe Gunnison shook his head. 'It ain't that yo're chewin' on, Randy. Yo're just a shade too anxious to shape my thinkin', an' a shade too shore I'm stupid enough to be swayed by yu.'

Randolph Gunnison's eyes began to shift warily. What was the old fool leading up to?

'Another question, then,' continued Lafe Gunnison remorselessly. 'What makes yu so shore I didn't hire Cameron myself?'

The panic welled into Randy Gunnison's eyes and he shrank back in his chair.

'Why ... I know you didn't ... wouldn't do anything like...' Randy licked his lips desperately. 'You're mad! What's wrong with you? Why are you asking me all these questions? You've no right...'

Lafe Gunnison advanced upon his cringing son. Muscles swelled in his neck and shoulders as the anger built in him.

'Tell me, damn yore eyes!' he roared. 'How are yu so shore?'

'I'm ... you're not ... I don't know what you mean,' squealed the younger man. 'You're mad! What are you saying? I only said what I heard...'

Lafe Gunnison grabbed his son's shirt in a hand like a

side of beef, and hauled Randolph Gunnison up until his son's toes were almost off the ground, handling him as if he were a small boy. The old man's face was suffused with anger.

'Who told yu?' he thundered. 'Who said it?'

His ham-like hand slapped Randy's face, leaving a red weal across the cheekbone. Randy's head swung to the left, to be slashed back again by the returning hand. Another right, and then backhand left brought tears of rage into Randolph Gunnison's eyes and a spittle of hatred formed at the corners of his split mouth.

'Tell—me—damn—yu! How—are—yu—so—shore?'

Hatred and venomous fear boiled in the younger Gunnison's heart. 'He'll kill me!' was his desperate thought as he struggled ineffectually to free himself from his father's iron grasp. 'Damn you, let go of me!' he shrilled. Lafe Gunnison ignored his son's protests, shaking him like a rat, and his right hand rose again to deliver yet another series of those stunning blows. It never landed. With a snake-like twist Randy reached beneath his coat and whipped from beneath his arm a deadly little snub-nosed Derringer pistol. Almost without volition he thrust it against his father's body and pulled the trigger. The noise of the shot was muffled, but the old man lurched backwards as if he had been hit with a sledgehammer, and fell with a crash which seemed to rock the house. Smoke rose from the scorched shirt. He did not move.

Like a trapped animal, sobs tearing at his throat, Randy leaped towards the window. His first hasty glance at the open yard revealed no sign of any of the men, and he realised with a thrill of fear and excitement that they were out on the range, that apart from the cook there was no one around. He stood stock still, listening like a hunted beast. There was no sound from the kitchen. The cook was probably in one of the other buildings. If . . . his mind cast wildly about for ideas while his eyes fell upon the sprawled body of his father on the floor.

'Yu damned interfering old fool,' he snarled. 'Now we'll see who's going to run the Sabre!'

He had hardly said the words when the sound of hoofbeats struck dread into his black heart. Mouthing a terrible oath, he sprang once more to the window. There, cantering into the yard, he recognised the Marshal of Yavapai, Tom Appleby.

CHAPTER SIXTEEN

THERE had been a grim council of war at the Harris ranch. After Appleby had left, Sudden had learned for the first time of the murder of Johnstone and Newley. Harris was deeply distressed not only by the terrible blow that the news of his friends' death had been but by the behaviour of the Marshal, which had resulted in Sudden expelling the lawman from the JH.

'I ain't suggestin' yu didn't do the right thing, Jim,' said Harris, a deep frown on his face. 'On'y now we ain't even got a friend in court. If Sabre chooses to ride all over us in Yavapai I'm bettin' Tom will turn a blind eye.'

'That being so, I'm thinkin' he was no friend in the first place,' put in Taylor.

'Alex is right,' added Kitson. 'If Tom Appleby is the kind o' man to let an affair o' this nature interfere with the way he does his job, then we're a sight better off on our own.'

'I'm just a wee bit concerned about Terry sendin' his man into town to bring back the bodies. . . .' Alex Taylor said after a pause. 'If Tom Appleby is as mean as ye all seem to think, then the poor chap oughtn't to go in alone. That Cameron would find him easy meat, I'm guessin'.'

Jake Harris got to his feet and replenished his cup from the pot on the stove.

'Those boys was my friends,' he announced. 'I'll go in for their bodies myself. I want to see they're buried decent.'

There was a chorus of disagreement and much dismay at this statement. Harris shook his head.

'If I don't go, folks are goin' to say we was too yeller to bury our dead,' Jake said. 'I got my pride, too.'

'That'll look right handsome on yore tombstone,' Sudden interjected flatly.

Harris flushed. 'Yu ain't got no call to talk to me like that, Jim,' he protested.

Sudden nodded, a smile making his next words disarming.

'Jake, yo're tryin' to do the right thing, an' I respect that. But yu got to admit that Philadelphia in there could probably give yu a head start an' outdraw yu. What chance do yu reckon yu'd have agin someone like Cameron?'

Alex Taylor nodded in agreement with Sudden's words. 'Aye, they're a breed o' scum, these gunfighters. All the same. Cold killers, without so much as a breath o' decency in their bodies. Yon Cameron'll no doubt be struttin' about Yavapai, free as air, boastin' his deeds. An' no doubt cuttin' a couple more notches on his gun butts.' He spat loudly. 'Scum!'

Sudden's face was cold and hard, and he stood abruptly. There was, had any of them noticed it, a hint of pain in his eyes, but he quickly concealed it beneath hooded lids and spoke to his employer.

'Yu talk to Shorty. Get the full story outa him. He can prove Randy an' Dancy is up to their necks in somethin', but I ain't quite figgered what, yet.'

Harris looked at Sudden in surprise. 'Yu goin' somewhere?' he asked.

A faint smile touched the corners of Sudden's mouth. 'I'm goin' to play a hunch. If what I think is right, then we're going to be mighty close to knowin' who's behind all this trouble.'

'Yu mean Gunnison?' asked Taylor.

'Lafe Gunnison? I don't know for shore,' replied Sudden. 'I'm thinkin' he knows as much as yu do, Alex, about the whole thing. Mebbe less.'

With those words he left Taylor staring at his retreating back with open mouth. When Sudden had closed the door behind him he turned to the others.

'I've heard some things said in my time that I've not understood,' he complained. 'But if Lafe Gunnison knows less than I do about what's been happenin' in this valley, then I reckon he must be one step short o' deaf! 'Cause I don't know a thing!'

CHAPTER SEVENTEEN

SUDDEN's face was set as he left the Harris house, walking around the side of the building to the corral where Nigger awaited. Gradually his tension eased, and he managed a smile. 'Oughta be used to bein' called names by now,' he told himself ruefully. 'Still gets under my skin, somehow.' He paused as he approached the window of Philadelphia's bedroom, and after a moment's thought, tapped on it. It was opened from inside by Susan Harris. Sudden could see Philadelphia leaning outwards from the bed to see who it was. He grinned at the cocked revolver in the youngster's hand.

'Don't shoot,' he smiled. 'I'm one o' them friendly Injuns.'

'All look the same to me,' scowled Philadelphia. 'Where yu gallivantin' off to now, Jim?'

'Got me a mite o' ridin' to do,' he told them both. 'How's the patient, ma'am?'

'Insists he's well enough to walk,' she said, a touch of asperity in her voice. 'Such nonsense. I actually found him up, out of bed, when I came in this morning.'

Philadelphia grinned unabashedly. 'Heck, I c'n stand if I got to. I shore ain't in no hurry, though.' His teasing smile brought roses into Susan's cheeks and she made a playful slap at his head which he ducked without ceasing to smile.

'Afore I go,' Green said. 'I forgot to tell yore Pa somethin', an' I'd ruther not go back in ... tell him not to send the Swede into Yavapai. Tell him I'll bring Reb an' Stan's bodies home.'

Philadelphia sat up, his eyebrows high on his forehead. 'Jim, yu can't go in alone. Let me come with yu. Or take some o' the others....' He trailed off as Sudden shook his head.

'Don't tell yore Pa till I've left,' he admonished Susan.

She nodded acceptance of this condition, with only a murmured, 'Good luck, Jim.'

He smiled at her. 'I'll be back around nightfall,' he said. 'Tell 'em in there not to shoot afore they see the whites o' my eyes.'

Then he was gone, leaving the girl biting her lip. She closed the window slowly and turned to ask her patient a question.

'Don't yu worry none,' he told her. 'Jim's a good man. If he says he'll be back at nightfall, he'll be back.'

And to himself he added, 'I shore hope I'm right.'

* * *

It took Sudden less than half an hour to get to Johnstone's place. Dust lay thick on the furniture and shelves, and a rat scurried across the floor as he entered the back room. The Virginian's house was a small one, with a large living-room, a bedroom, and a lean-to at the back of the house where Johnstone had kept all his bridles, saddle, and other implements for use on the farm. With the shovel which he had brought along Sudden tested the dirt floor. Across the room in parallel lines he moved, slowly chunking the blade of the tool into the ground as deeply as he could, repeating the process every six inches or so. He worked away steadily for nearly an hour before the sound of the shovel entering the earth changed slightly. He straightened, nodded, bent to his task. The sweat poured off him as he turned the earth, hard packed from years of pounding. In another hour he had found what he wanted, filled in the hole, and sluiced cold water over his grimy face and arms. Then, his face grim, he saddled up again and pointed Nigger south for Yavapai. The recent rains had washed the prairies emerald green, and larks carolled their way to heaven as he passed threateningly close to their hidden nests. The puncher saw none of this. His mind was occupied with dark thoughts that blinded him to the beauty of the day.

He reached the town of Yavapai shortly before two o'clock. His eyes were narrowed and his air preoccupied. A pattern of villainy so immense was appearing that it seemed almost unbelievable, and yet it was the only theory which fitted the events and the facts he knew.

He rode directly to the squat adobe building which housed the Yavapai Valley Bank, spending almost an hour in the locked office of Granger, the manager. Granger accompanied Sudden to the door when he left, a worried expression on his normally bland face.

'I do hope I've done right, Mr. Green,' he said, wringing his hands.

'Yu write them letters to the men whose names I gave yu,' the puncher told him. 'Yu'll find they'll back me up. I'm obliged for all yore help. In the meantime, yu'll keep what I told yu to yoreself, o' course.'

'But of course, Mr. Green,' protested Granger. 'It has always been our policy to——'

'That's fine,' seh,' Sudden broke in. 'Yu'll excuse me.'

His jaw set. Rarely had he ever set out to deliberately push another human being beyond the borderline, to provoke him deliberately into a fight; but he knew that there would be no other way. Cameron was a festering sore, and he had to be excised. Sudden knew it, but the thought gave him no pleasure. With a measured stride he walked up the street towards Tyler's.

CHAPTER EIGHTEEN

TYLER bustled up the length of the bar as Sudden entered the saloon, drying his hands upon the striped apron he always wore.

'Green, ain't it?' he asked. 'Ain't seen yu in town since yu collided with Jim Dancy. Yu been workin' up on the Mesquites, I heard.'

'Yu heard right,' Sudden told him as the bartender poured him a drink.

Tyler's hand was unsteady, and with his head down he murmured, 'Take my advice an' walk out o' here, Green. There's a feller in here run in with a couple o' yore people. If he knows yo're one o' them there'll be trouble.'

'Shucks, I ain't huntin' no trouble,' Sudden told him. 'I just come in to take the bodies back.' His voice had risen slightly as he spoke, and carried far enough for the men at the far end of the bar to hear his words. Sudden noticed a man look up suddenly at the sound of his voice, and from the description Jake and Philadelphia had given him, knew that this was Wes Cameron. He did not reveal that he had noticed the gunman, however, but remained staring down into his drink.

Cameron's voice cut coldly through the low murmur of conversation which stilled abruptly at his words.

'Well, well, a pilgrim! Step up, stranger, an' I'll buy yu a drink.'

Sudden shook his head. 'I got one,' he said shortly.

Cameron's expression changed, and his cronies backed away uneasily as he bent his cold gaze upon the unconcerned cowboy.

'When Wes Cameron offers yu a drink, mister, yu better take it!'

Sudden turned slowly to face Cameron. Then, as if thinking better of something, he shrugged, and returned to gazing moodily into his glass. The sheer effrontery of his gesture was not lost upon the spectators, most of whom awaited Cameron's reaction with bated breath. One or two, however, remembered this tall, slow-smiling man. One such leaned over to his neighbour and whispered, 'That's the jasper had the run-in with Jim Dancy.'

'He must be crazy, talkin' that way to Cameron!' the other said.

'Mebbe,' retorted the first speaker. 'He don't look it, though.'

Indeed, the puncher looked the complete picture of unconcern as he leaned, elbows on the bar, frowning into his drink.

Cameron elbowed his way through the knot of men at the bar and stopped two feet from Sudden.

'People usually look at me when I'm talkin' to them,' the gunman snarled poisonously.

Green half turned, insolently eyed Cameron from head to foot, and said, with a brutal clarity which carried right across the room, 'Must be 'cause yu got such charmin' manners.'

There was a scrabble of feet and chair legs as the onlookers in the bar moved hurriedly out of the possible line of fire. Surely this insolent cowpuncher could not continue to talk to Cameron thus and live?

'Ain't I seen yu somewheres?' Cameron said. He was puzzled by the complete lack of response to his name that this saturnine individual was showing, and somewhere in his brain a faint warning bell was ringing. There was something familiar about the man, but what? He shrugged away the feeling as Sudden replied:

'Not if I seen yu first.'

A murmur arose from the onlookers, and Cameron swelled with rage as he heard it. Cameron's face was livid with rage; all of Yavapai hung on his next words.

'Yu better watch yore lip, stranger! Yu know who I am?'

All sound stopped as Sudden replied, 'On'y Wes Cameron I ever heard of was a lily-livered coyote who shot down farmers, kids, an' young girls. I heard he was the kind who's sell the straw outa his mother's kennel.' He turned to face the gaping gunman, all trace of his former lounging stance gone. 'Now that wouldn't be yu, would it?'

For a single instant Cameron stood stock still. Then the rage roared into his brain and with an oath he clawed for the gun at his side. What happened next was to become a legend in Yavapai. Cameron's gun was not even clear of the cut-away holster when the barrel of Sudden's revolver touched the gunman's nose, while the puncher's left hand stopped the reflex upward action of Cameron's unfinished draw. Cameron froze, a cold slimy finger of fear probing his heart. He knew that if he so much as blinked an eyelid this cold, slit-eyed devil who had outdrawn him so incredibly could, with every justification in the world, shoot him down. The killing light in his opponent's eyes confirmed it. Cameron did not move as the puncher gritted, 'Let go o' yore gun!'

Cameron's hand relaxed and the revolver slid back into its ornate scabbard, while every breath in the saloon was expelled in a gusty sigh.

'My Gawd! did yu see that?' gasped the man who had earlier identified Green.

'Damned if I did,' his table companion told him. 'I never even seen him move!'

Sudden stepped back, covering Cameron. He surveyed the gunman coldly.

'Killin's too good for a polecat like yu,' he grated. 'Shuck yore belt.'

A faint gleam, half puzzlement, half triumph, appeared in Cameron's eyes. He unbuckled the heavy, stitched belt, which fell to the sanded floor with a thump. At Sudden's command he stepped away from it. Still keeping Cameron covered, Sudden kicked the gunbelt across the floor away from the gunman. He then took two steps backwards, holstering the gun he had drawn so unbelievably swiftly. His hands reached for the buckle of his own gunbelt.

'Killin' yu'd be too easy,' he said. 'I reckon yu got to be shown the hard way that all farmers ain't such easy marks.'

He handed the gunbelt to the bartender, who accepted it open-mouthed, then faced Cameron once more.

'Yu reckon we're even matched now, Cameron? Or is hittin' defenceless young girls more in yore line o' country?'

Cameron had watched his opponent's actions with disbelief, hardly able to comprehend his good fortune. He was well versed in the dirtier forms of saloon brawling, and the murderous tactics employed to maim, blind, or cripple an opponent in a fist fight. This fool with the incredible draw had played right into his hands! Instead of his reputation being destroyed, the gunman could recoup his ascendancy with no real loss of face. He had weighed the build of the nester, and knew that he had the advantage of weight and reach, although Green was taller. These thoughts flashed through his head as the dark-haired cowboy turned to face him, and with a cry of inarticulate rage Cameron threw himself upon his enemy.

Sudden, however, had seen the move coming and moved lightly aside, allowing Cameron's blundering body to pass him between the bar and his left side. As the gunman's head dropped, Green laced his hands together and dealt Cameron a sickening blow over the ear which chopped the man to the floor, splitting his lips open. Cameron rose, spitting sand and blood from his mouth, and from the crouch leaped once more at Sudden. Once again the cowboy moved back and to the side, and once more the brutal chopping blow stretched Cameron face down on the floor.

Everyone in the saloon was on his feet now and forming a close-packed, jostling ring about the two fighting men. Yells of encouragement, criticism, and advice spewed from the men as Cameron got to his feet, more slowly this time, and eyed Sudden more warily. He shook his head, pulled his body upright, and once more charged at the slim form before him, ready this time for the evasive movement he expected Sudden to make. The puncher made no such move, but instead his left arm came out as straight as a ramrod, with all the force of his supple body behind it. Cameron ran right into the punch and reeled sideways into the arms of the crowd.

'Give 'em more room!' somebody yelled.

'Yeah, Cameron's got nowhere to fall down!' was the rejoinder, one which brought the blood to Cameron's face and sent him circling forward, more cautiously this time, changing the form of his attack. This time it was Sudden who stepped forward, almost into the enveloping bear-hug that Cameron tried to use. Faster than the eye could follow, Sudden's fists thudded into the gunman's face, drawing a gout of blood from the man's nose.

'Stan' still an' fight, damn yore eyes!' Cameron cursed, but his unmarked opponent merely grinned coldly and then, light on his feet, buried a further flurry of blows in the gunman's middle. Cameron folded slightly, his breath heavier.

'Hell,' cried one disgusted spectator, 'this ain't a fight, it's a massacree.'

'Yu want to step in here an' try?' ground out Cameron, hearing the insult.

'Couldn't do much worse,' was the contemptuous reply.

Cameron shook his head to clear it. Although Green's blows had been punishing, they had not hurt him as much as he was trying to make it appear. If he could get this smiling devil to drop his guard for a moment... Without warning he dived forward at Sudden, landing a heavy blow on the puncher's temple. Sudden, momentarily stunned by the blow, was unable to evade the groping grip of the gunman, whose knee came up wickedly, dropping Sudden gasping to the floor. Sudden managed to roll desperately aside as Cameron's spurred boot came stamping down upon the ground where a second before his head had been. A cold rage flooded into Sudden's body, and in a smooth movement he rolled over and up on to his feet. Gone now was any pretence of avoiding Cameron's rushes. He disregarded the gunman's attempts at self-defence and attack and went after the man, trading blow for sickening blow, taking whatever Cameron threw at him and hurling his own blood-spattered fists at the leering visage.

The sweat-stained, battered principles, encircled by the brutal faces of the onlookers eager to see every moment, every blow struck; the flat sound of bone on flesh, the wounded grunts when body blows went home; these, under the flaring lights greyed by the fog of smoke, dulled by the curses of the crowd, created a picture which would have defied the descriptive powers of a Dante.

Sudden knew that it was madness to fight like this, but the primitive urge to destroy this man with his bare fists had, for once, overcome his patience. Dominated by his intention to beat this killer into the dust he took blow upon blow that might have been avoided, for the satisfaction of once more battering his own fists into the torn face of his opponent.

It had to end. No two men could go on with such brutal punishment and stand. A chance blow from Cameron sent Sudden reeling backwards against the bar, and before he could straighten, Cameron was upon him, twisting, thrashing, trying desperately to hold the puncher there. Sudden was conscious of the hand clawing his face, the seeking thumb searching to blind him. A surge of fury possessed him and he smashed his fist blindly forward. It caught Cameron just below the chin, in his corded neck. Gasping, clawing at his throat, trying desperately to breathe, Cameron fell backwards, momentarily paralysed.

'Yu got him, mister!' yelled one of the onlookers. 'Whale the hell out'n him!'

Sudden shook his head; weak and dizzy, he stood waiting for Cameron to regain his feet. He knew that the shouted advice had been eminently sensible, and fully in accord with what Cameron would have done had the situation been reversed. But he did not fight that way. Cameron was recovering. His breath rasped in his throat as he climbed once more to his feet.

'That was a sucker play,' he croaked. 'Now I'm gonna kill yu!'

His head dropped, and he rushed in, all science gone, his arm shooting forward to deliver a blow, which, had it landed, would have ended the contest then and there. But Sudden had been ready for just such a move, and acting too swiftly for those watching to follow, he grasped the descending wrist and, using Cameron's own force and weight, twisted around like a pivot. Pulled forward by Sudden's unexpected move, Cameron hit the puncher's thigh and went up into the air. Sudden released his grip and Cameron shot forward to land with a crash full length at the end of the bar where he had originally stood. For some moments he lay there, supine, senseless, only the heaving chest showing that he still lived. Slowly, one eye opened, then the other. The realisation that he had been bested by the slim, battered man who stood watching him warily flooded into him, and in that same moment a flash of recognition came to him.

'My Gawd!' he gasped. 'Now I know yu! Yo're that Texas outlaw! Yo're—Sudden!'

Sudden! This stunning revelation brought a gasp from the onlookers, and the unbelievable wizardry they had witnessed was in one word fully explained to them. So this was Sudden, the daredevil whose name was legend throughout the Southwest! No wonder he had outdrawn Wes Cameron! Probably no other man could have!

Cameron levered himself up on to one elbow. A fury of hatred shook him, and he shot a glance sideways. His gun and belt lay within arm's length.

'Yu lose, Sudden!' he screamed.

In one rolling movement Cameron had reached his gun, and his hand was clawing at the butt when a shot roared out and Sudden, who stood unarmed and helpless, his own guns behind Tyler's bar, whirled to see Tom Appleby standing just inside the batwing doors, smoke dribbling from the muzzle of his forty-five.

Cameron fell backwards, a look of shock and malevolence upon his face. He half rose again upon his elbow, a quivering hand trying to line the gun-barrel on Appleby. 'Yu ... double ... cr——' Appleby's gun blazed again, and Cameron was slammed backwards, his face still fixed in a scowl of hatred. One of the watchers bent over the prostrate form, then straightened, shaking his head.

'Cashed,' he announced to all and sundry. 'An' good riddance!'

'Amen to that!' seconded Tyler. 'Tom, yu arrove just in time.'

'Ain't so shore,' said Appleby coldly. 'How did it start?'

Eager voices supplied him with the details of what had passed, losing nothing in the telling. While the patrons of the bar clamoured around the lawman to add to his knowledge their own story, their own opinions, Appleby's cold eyes never left Sudden. Nodding, he shouldered his way through the knot of men surrounding him and came across to the bar, where Sudden was buckling on his gunbelt once more.

'So yo're Sudden,' he said. 'Mebbe I'd a' done this town a service if I'd let Cameron kill yu. Then I could o' hung him an' rid the world o' two o' yu.'

Sudden faced the lawman calmly, his face unreadable. 'Yu just saved my life, Appleby,' he said quietly. 'I'm overlookin' what yu said.'

'Don't,' Appleby said shortly. 'Yo're one o' the lawless breed an' yu ain't wanted in Yavapai!'

He turned and faced the crowd in the saloon. Holding up his arms for silence, he addressed them in grave tones.

'Afore yu all start tellin' me I've gone loco, lissen to me: there's worse news tonight than one rat killin' another.' He glanced malevolently over his shoulder at

Sudden. 'Mebbe this jasper knows about it, too. I just come in from the Sabre. Randy Gunnison's old man's hoss came in this afternoon with blood on the saddle.'

A roar of excited speculation greeted this announcement. One man stepped forward with a question.

'Yu got any idee where Gunnison was headin' when he left Sabre, Tom?'

'Randy sez he was ridin' up into the Mesquites,' the lawman told him.

'He rode up thar alone?' asked a puzzled bystander.

'So I'm told,' Appleby said. 'He told Randy that he aimed to have a man-to-man talk with Jake Harris afore things got too far out o' hand in the valley. Knowed if he rode up there with his crew the nesters'd reckon it was a war party an' commence firin'. So he went in alone.'

'Yu reckon someone's bushwhacked ol' Lafe?' asked Tyler, his eyes wide.

'I'm hopin' not,' Appleby said coldly. 'Or this jasper an' his friends up in the Mesquites is goin' to have some explainin' to do.'

All eyes swung to fix upon Sudden, who had listened to this news with as much surprise as any man in the place. Sudden fixed Appleby with a flat stare.

'Yu aimin' to make arrests or preside at a lynchin'?' he snapped.

'Neither—yet!' was the sneering reply. 'Tomorrow mornin', however, I'm goin' to comb the Mesquites with a posse. If we find out that anythin' has happened to Lafe Gunnison we'll be asking yu an' yore friends a few leadin' questions, an' yu can bet yore last cent on that!'

An ugly murmur among the crowd convinced Green that the lawman had the sentiment of the townspeople behind him. Gunnison was a big man to these people, more important to their lives than any of the homesteaders or, indeed, all of them.

'I aim to collect Johnstone an' Newley's bodies,' he told the men who, instinct with menace, half circled about him. His voice was mild and devoid of emphasis. 'Then I'm takin' them out to the Mesquites. That's where I'll be if anyone wants me.' He said this last looking directly at Appleby, whose eyes fell before Sudden's. The onlookers watched this silent exchange, and when the puncher moved towards the door, fell back. Their faces were sullen, but they had no stomach for any trouble with this hard-eyed, acid-tongued individual who had already proven his mettle before their astonished eyes.

As the batwing doors flapped behind him a hubbub of speculation began. The onlookers bellied up to Tyler's bar, and the comments flew thick and fast.

'Sudden, huh? He's a killer, shore enough,' said one man.

'Shore he is,' scoffed Tyler. 'That's why he beefed Cameron when he had 'im dead to rights. If that boy's a killer I'm a Dutchman.'

'Yeah, well give us some drinks here, Dutchy,' roared a man at the far end of the bar, raising a long laugh from the others. The humour was rough, for they were mostly men who lived hard, whose life was harsh. Easily swayed, they had been Cameron's while he had held the town in his hand, and Sudden's when he toppled the gunman. Now, as the arguments about the legendary career of the Southwestern gunfighter and what they had seen him do that night raged, so did the balance of opinion shift forward and back.

Listening to them, his lips curled in contempt, the Marshal of Yavapai laughed to himself; they could be swayed again.

CHAPTER NINETEEN

'Yu complete, utter, damn' fool! Yu stupid idjut! I orta beat yu to a pulp!'

Had any of the respected citizens of Yavapai seen their Marshal at this moment, as he paced the floor of the Sabre ranchhouse living-room like a caged panther, their jaws would have dropped with astonishment. If it had then been possible for them to see the object of the Marshal's vitriolic scorn their confusion would have been complete. Randy Gunnison cowered before the terrible wrath of the slit-eyed lawman, occasionally letting his frightened gaze wander towards Jim Dancy, who was sitting in the big leather armchair watching Randy Gunnison's discomfiture with savage enjoyment.

'I couldn't do anything else,' whimpered Randy. 'He'd cottoned on, I'm telling you.'

'Tell me what he said.'

'I told you once.'

'Tell me again. Every detail. An' by God! yu'd better not leave anythin' out!'

Once again the scion of the Gunnison family related the details which had led to his shooting the old man. As he spoke, his eyes wandered as if drawn by magnets to the window, through which he could see the wagon outside the ranch. A tarpaulin loosely covered the huddled heap which was his father's body; Appleby had wasted no time after his arrival.

'He damn' well bluffed yu, Randy,' grated Appleby. 'He couldn't have known anything! If yu hadn't been so spineless, this—ah! it ain't no use frettin' on that. The question is, what do we do now?'

'Looks like we try to pin it on Harris, far as I see it,' put in Dancy.

Appleby nodded, preoccupied. 'Yo're right, I was thinkin' the same thing. The question is: how?'

'Well, the answer better come quick,' Dancy retorted. 'The hands'll be in off the range in an hour or two.'

Appleby nodded again. His evil mind was working furiously, and he paced restlessly backwards and forwards as he thought, a scowl of concentration upon his face. After a few more minutes he stopped.

'I think I've got it!' he exulted. 'Listen, Jim. If yu see any holes in it, pull me up sharp. I think I've got a way to pin it on that bunch an' make it stick. It'll need some quick work. Here's how I see it: Jim, yu get the old man's hoss saddled up an' take it with yu an' the wagon. Kill somethin'—coyote, some varmint, anythin'll do—an' smear blood on the saddle. When yu get to the Yavapai, turn him loose. Make shore he's got plenty o' marks on him to show he's been across the river. Then take the old man's body up into the Mesquites, near as yu can get to the Harris place. Don't be seen, yu hear? That could be —fatal.'

He paused to let the words sink in, and Dancy nodded. Randy sat forward, his eyes gleaming with interest.

'Tip the body into a canyon—somewhere nobody'll find it without a real hard search. Then spill some blood where it can be seen. Yu, Randy—what'd the old man carry no matter where he was goin'?'

'Yu mean ... oh ... his watch. Gun. Wallet. Things like that.'

Appleby turned to Dancy. 'Use his gun. Fire a shot out of it. Leave it where it can be found, near the blood-stains. Scuff the ground up, but keep on hard ground when yo're leavin'—I don't want no tracks up there any-one can foller back here.'

Dancy nodded. 'Easy so far,' he growled. 'What was the old man doin' up in the Mesquites?'

'I already thought of that,' interjected Randy eagerly. 'I can say he told me he wanted to go up an' talk to Harris, man to man.'

'Wouldn't've gone alone, though,' said Appleby thoughtfully.

'That's easy, too, Tom,' Randy told him. 'He said he figgered if he rode up there with some o' the crew they'd expect he'd come for war, and act accordingly. He said he was going to go alone to make sure there was no trouble ... how does that sound?'

'Sounds fair,' admitted Dancy. 'I can't see no holes in it.'

'What do we do next?' pursued Randy.

'We sit an' wait until the hoss gets back. Then I go into town an' raise a posse. We ride into the Mesquites tomorrow, find the sign, an' pay Harris a visit.' He fingered his chin thoughtfully. 'I got a score to settle there, anyway.'

'So we pin it on the nesters,' Dancy said. 'We still got to prove one o' them did it. They might all have alibis.'

'For a whole day?' scoffed Appleby. 'One o' them at least has had to be out o' the house long enough to have done it. An' anyway'—he leered—'who else would'a' done it?'

Dancy slapped his thigh, an evil smile creasing his face.

'I got to hand it to yu, Tom! Yu shore got it worked out sweet. Yu want me any more?'

'No. Get on with it. An' remember—don't fail me.' The words were quietly spoken, but the threat behind them did not fail to register upon the burly Sabre foreman.

'Hell, I got as much to lose as yu,' he protested. 'I'll take care o' things real smooth. Don't yu fret none.'

In a moment the two men heard him clamber aboard the wagon, and through the window saw the Sabre man hazing the team off down the trail towards the river. Appleby whirled to confront Randy Gunnison.

'Yu better pray we pull this off,' he gritted. 'If anythin' goes wrong yu'll—regret it.'

'It'll be all right, Tom,' Randy said, smiling fawningly. 'It might even speed things up. That isn't too bad, is it?'

'Wait an' see,' the Marshal told him coldly. 'I got other worries.' Randy looked his question, and Appleby exclaimed impatiently, 'Gawd, yo're stupid! If Lafe Gunnison could start wonderin' who brought Wes Cameron into Yavapai, yu think that Green feller won't have had the same question stuck in his craw? We can damn shore assume he knows Harris ain't responsible, an' if it occurs to him that mebbe Lafe didn't bring Wes in neither he won't take long to put two an' two together.'

Randy's expression grew apprehensive once more.

'Yu mean—Cameron might talk?'

'He might,' was the meaningful reply. 'I reckon I'd better make shore he don't.' His words put a shiver down the listener's spine.

'I thought you said Cameron was under control? If he were to talk...' Randy Gunnison's face was drawn with fear at the prospect, and Appleby laughed savagely.

'If yo're so worried, why don't yu ride in to Yavapai an' fix it so he can't?'

'You're not serious, Tom. I couldn't——'

'Damn right, yu couldn't, yu spineless jellyfish!' snapped Tom Appleby. 'An' don't yu forget it. Cameron'll be—taken care of.' His face was malignant, lit with evil. 'In case yu ever think o' steppin' out o' line, remember this: yu ain't indispensable any more. Lafe

Gunnison is dead. Sabre is mine. Yu jest cancelled yore life insurance.'

Randy Gunnison looked at the lawman with eyes as empty as ice in a bucket. The dreadful realisation of the power which the lawman had over him came all the more shockingly as the words struck home. It was true. Now that his father was dead, Appleby had no more need of him ... unless ...

'Yu'd better wait until you're sure your scheme has worked, Tom,' he said, as firmly as he dared.

Appleby eyed him with contempt, only a faint curiosity in his voice as he said, 'Is that so?'

'You may need the Sabre yet. If you have to get the nesters out of the Mesquites by force, Sabre riders will have to do it. And you'll need me to tell them to do it.'

Appleby's expression changed, and a warm smile appeared on his face.

'Hell, Randy,' he said, clapping him on the shoulder, 'I guess I spoke out o' turn, at that! You orta know I'm strung up a mite over this business. Hell, yu're a big part o' my plans. Yu an' me an' Jim, we're in this together.'

Completely deceived by this complete change of mood, Randy Gunnison warmed once more to the man who so completely controlled his destiny.

'By God, Tom,' he enthused, 'I can't wait till we get that money and I can leave this rotten valley! I only wish we didn't have to wait. I'd go tomorrow if I could!'

'Don't yu fret none,' Appleby assured him. 'When we take the pot, I am to make shore yu get yores first.'

And so besotted by the thought of the money earned by falsehood, betrayal, and murder was Randolph Gunnison that he completely missed the possible double meaning of the lawman's final words.

CHAPTER TWENTY

THE morning following Sudden's return from Yavapai was a gloomy one at the Harris ranch. The puncher had related in brief phrases the events of the preceding night, and while the death of Cameron had been discussed only as a matter of grim satisfaction, the further blow of Gunnison's disappearance brought concern to the brows of Sudden's listeners.

'Dammit, but that's bad news, Jim!' exclaimed Harris. 'Who d'yu reckon could be behind such a thing?'

Sudden told him of the remarks Appleby had made, and the old homesteader burst out, 'But that's damnable! Yu mean he accused yu o' bein' implicated?'

'Let's say he didn't mention anyone else by name, an' leave it at that,' the puncher responded. 'I would'a' said that yore Marshal was keener on stirrin' up trouble than he is on dampin' it down.'

'Oh, Jim, I can't believe that Appleby's serious,' interposed Taylor. 'You're likely misreadin' what he said.'

'Mebbe,' Sudden said non-committally. 'I wish he'd 'a' held fire on Cameron, though. I wanted a long talk with that jasper.'

'Yu think he might o' talked?'

'We'll never know now,' rejoined Sudden quietly.

They turned in early, and in the morning rose to the unhappy task of burying their dead neighbours. During Sudden's absence two graves had been dug on a grassy knoll a little distance from the Harris house, and the homesteaders stood bare-headed beside the graves as the Virginian and his friend were lowered into the earth. Alex Taylor read a passage from the Bible, and they returned to a silent breakfast.

The sound of approaching horses dispelled their lethargy and within moments they were at their posts by window and door, guns at the ready. They saw Tom Appleby lead a group of about twenty men into the yard. The lawman hailed the house. Taylor pointed out the presence of Randy Gunnison among the riders, as Harris lifted the bar of the door and stepped out into the open. He cradled his shotgun across his burly forearm and faced the lawman.

Inside the house a quick word from Sudden had sent Shorty scurrying to hide in the bedroom. The tall puncher quickly told the others to keep the little miner's presence a secret should anyone enter the house; he had his own reasons for not letting anyone from Yavapai see

Shorty—yet. Taylor and Kitson caught his drift immediately.

'If what he says about Randy Gunnison is true, the more he keeps outa sight the better his health'll stay,' Kitson remarked grimly.

Jake Harris spoke to Appleby.

'Marshal,' he began. His voice was quite neutral. 'What is this?'

Behind him Sudden moved into the doorway, where he leaned almost negligently against the door-frame. Only a close watcher would have noticed that at no time were his hands further than a few inches away from the black butts of his holstered revolvers.

'A posse, all sworn in an' legal!' was Appleby's clarion reply to the homesteader's question. 'So tell yore men to lay down their guns, Jake. Any trouble an' it'll go hard with yu men.'

Harris made no move to comply with the lawman's command, and Appleby flushed slightly.

'Yore man there tell yu it looked like Lafe Gunnison's been murdered?' he demanded harshly.

Harris nodded. 'He told us. I guess we was shocked. I don't reckon any of us was upset. An' it don't tell me what yo're doin' ridin' up here with twenty men.'

'I'm doin' what has to be done,' said Appleby, harshly. 'I got to ask yu some questions. We been lookin' around in the hills since sunup. We found some bloodstains, an' Lafe Gunnison's forty-five, with a shot fired. Ground churned up some, but no tracks we could foller.'

'Yu ain't found his body?'

'No sign of it. If he was bushwhacked, which I figger he must'a' been, the killer could've hidden the body somewhere that'd take us a month to find. It looks pretty bad to me.'

'Jim told me Lafe was ridin' up here to see me, accordin' to young Gunnison, there.'

'That's what he told me, Harris!' came Randy Gunnison's spiteful voice.

'Wal, he never arrove,' said Jake finally. 'There's plenty o' men here to back what I say.'

Appleby nodded. 'Never thought he did,' he said. 'I figger he got no further than where we found the blood.

My guess is he ran into someone who mebbe argued with him about somethin'. There was a fight; Lafe got a shot in afore the killer dropped him.'

'Who would'a' wanted to kill Gunnison?' asked Harris. 'I swear I——'

'Don't make any difference what you swear, Harris,' cut in Randy Gunnison. 'You could deny it on a Bible, but everyone in this valley knows you would have been glad to see my father dead, and so would your nester friends!'

Appleby half turned in his saddle.

'Watch yore lip, Randy!' he said, an edge in his voice. The rancher's son bit his lip and relapsed into sullen silence. The Marshal turned again to face Harris.

'Jake, things look bad up here. I know I upset yore gal the last time I was here, but right now I got a job to do, an' I got to tell yu: things look bad for yu.'

'For me? What do yu mean, for me?' roared the old man. 'I ain't seen Gunnison in a coon's age!'

'Can yu account for yore friends between, say, nine an' eleven yestiddy mornin'?' He saw the old man's mouth set in a thin line, and held up a hand, Indian peace-sign fashion. 'Jake, don't get sore. I'm on'y askin' what I got to ask.'

His voice was reasonable, and the old homsteader nodded.

'I suppose yo're right,' he growled. 'Well, let me see. I was in the house all mornin'. Susie an' the boy could tell yu that.'

'By the same token, that lets them out,' nodded Appleby. 'Go on.'

'Alex an' Terry was over at the Lazy K, feedin' the stock. They left about mid-mornin'—mebbe eleven.'

'Times don't fit,' Appleby encouraged him. 'That lets them out. Gunnison was killed up near the trail to Yavapai.'

'Alex's boys is over on their own range. I misdoubt they went huntin' a man they didn't know was comin' here.'

Appleby nodded, his eyes resting on the lounging figure behind Harris. 'An' yore man Green?'

'I was on my way into town,' Green answered quietly.

A mutter issued from the possemen. Green's answer

placed him squarely in the area in which Gunnison had been murdered, and at approximately the right time.

'So yu could've met Gunnison up in the Mesquites?'

'I could've. But I didn't. I didn't even set eyes on Gunnison,' Sudden told Appleby.

'Hell, you could'a' done,' interrupted one of the possemen. 'Seems mighty strange yore ridin' into town an' takin' on that Cameron *hombre* the same day Gunnison is killed,' added another.

An unholy gleam of triumph lit Appleby's eyes. One of the townsmen, quite unwittingly, had given him the lead he needed, the key with which he could turn the lock of the resistance of the homesteaders. He managed to suppress his exulting feelings and asked Sudden, 'What time yu get to town yestiddy?'

'Aroun' two,' replied the puncher laconically. His mind was not idle; he was well aware of what the lawman was leading up to, and he thanked his stars that he had taken the precautionary steps that he already had.

'An yu left here . . . ?'

'Around eight.'

'What took yu so long?' pounced Appleby. 'It's on'y about three hours to town.'

'I made a detour,' explained Sudden. 'Took a look at the Johnstone an' Newley spreads to make shore things was okay over there.'

'Anyone see yu?' demanded one of the posse. Sudden shook his head.

'So we on'y got yore word for it,' gloated Appleby. 'At least an hour, mebbe two, missin'. Plenty o' time to have met Gunnison an' killed him.'

'Now hold on there, Tom,' protested Harris. 'Jim here had no reason to kill Lafe Gunnison!'

'I can give yu one,' hissed the Marshal. 'Randy had a sneakin' suspicion that Lafe brought this Cameron feller into Yavapai to drive yu an' yore neighbours out o' the Mesquites. I'm bettin' we'll find somethin' to prove it, too.'

'No bet,' said Sudden coldly. 'I'd guess it was goin' to be a shore thing.' His sardonic words brought Appleby's head around, and the venom was plain for all to see now.

'So: here's how it probably happened. Mr. Green here meets up with Gunnison. Gunnison an' him argue. Mebbe he accuses Gunnison o' hirin' Cameron to kill Johnstone an' Newley. Mebbe Lafe goes for his gun. An' this jasper kills him. Then he figgers he'll finish the whole job an' go into Yavapai an' pick a fight with Cameron.'

'He shorely done just that,' enjoined one of the posse, a big bearded man who had been in Tyler's saloon when Cameron had been killed. 'I seen the whole thing.'

'So, havin' mebbe got Lafe to admit he hired Cameron, this jasper here beats seven different kinds o' sugar out o' Cameron, but Cameron damn' near beefs him instead. I got there just in time to stop Cameron doin' murder, not knowin' who's involved. It's on'y after Cameron's dead I find out. Jake—yu know who this jasper is?'

'Shore, he's Jim Green,' Harris replied.

'Jim Green, Jim Green,' jeered Appleby. 'This *hombre*'s wanted for murder in Texas! He's got another name down there, ain't yu, Green? Or should I say "Sudden"?'

An astonished oath burst from the lips of one of Harris's neighbours inside. Kitson and Taylor came to the window to look, as if for the first time, at the smiling, quietly spoken man who was now revealed as the notorious Sudden.

'Hell, I knowed that!' laughed Harris, enjoying the consternation on the Marshal's face as he said it. 'He told me when I first hired him.'

Appleby regained his composure and his face was serious when he said, 'Jake, are yu tellin' me that yu knowingly hired a killer?' The expressions of his posse had turned grim and several of them were nodding significantly at each other. Too late, Harris realised how his words could be construed, but he was too proud to retract. He glared at the possemen defiantly, as the Marshal went on inexorably.

'Jake, an unkind man might figger yu'd hired this killer to do some dirty work for yu. He might even figger yu'd cut down Gunnison to make it easy to run a sandy over this valley, with someone like Mr. Sudden to do yore gunnin'.'

'An unkind man might get his teeth knocked in if it wasn't for the fact that my daughter's standing inside the house,' Harris told the lawman coldly. 'Yu better take them words back, Marshal.'

'Hell, I on'y said what some might say,' Appleby protested, his hands spread wide. 'I ain't sayin' that's what yu done!'

'Well, I knowed about Jim, an' I'm sayin' here an' now I don't believe half of what they say about Sudden is true.'

'That's as might be,' said Appleby pursing his lips. 'It ain't my decision. Green, I'm goin' to have to take yu in. Even if yu ain't the one killed Gunnison, yo're wanted by the Sheriff o' Fourways in Texas.'

Randy Gunnison spurred his horse forward.

'I reckon Yavapai's got the prior claim,' he shrilled. 'This—this scum will stand trial for murderin' my father!'

A rumble of agreement came from the riders massed behind the Marshal, and one or two of them even started forward towards Sudden. Appleby held up a hand to stop them.

'Yu better make no fuss, Green,' he told the indolent figure still leaning against the door-frame as though he had no part or interest in the events occurring before him. Sudden smiled and stood upright. His hands hung negligently near his tied-down guns, and his voice was deceptively mild as he spoke.

'I reckon I could drop yu an' mebbe six more afore yu got me,' he said. A jeering note entered his voice, and he half crouched, his eyes narrow, his very figure charged with menace. Randy Gunnison backed his horse away, and several of the possemen, who had already seen the incredible speed of this man's draw, knew that he was making no idle boast. Appleby, however, was unperturbed.

'Yo're probably right,' he told Sudden. 'On'y yu better think about what would happen to the kid in there—an' the girl—if yu open the ball.' He waited for these telling words to have their effect. Sudden straightened and the tenseness left his body. He could not take the risk.

'Yore trick, Marshal,' he said. 'But the game ain't over.'

Appleby's smile was malevolent. 'Yo're right,' he agreed. 'See if yu can win it on bluff.'

'Tom,' protested Harris, 'this is a damfool thing. Yu can't prove such a cock an' bull story in court!'

'I got a man who had the time, the opportunity, and the reason. Show me anyone else who fits the bill an' I'll go an' talk to him. Until then, yu better hold yore tongue. I ain't shore but what yu ain't deeper in this than yu say, Jake. I'm givin' yu the benefit o' considerable doubt.'

'I've seen men hung on less!' This from Randy Gunnison, his courage returning as Sudden seemed no longer menacing.

'Yo're makin' a mistake, Tom. A bad mistake,' Jake told the lawman.

'Ain't for me to decide,' Appleby retorted. 'Tell it to the jury. Now: yu Green! reach down nice an' easy, an' drop yore gunbelt. Then step away from it.'

He reinforced this order by drawing and cocking his gun. Sudden shrugged and did as he was bid, whereupon two of the possemen dismounted and bound his hands securely together.

'Get his hoss,' Appleby told another man. When Sudden was mounted, his hands were tied to the pommel of the saddle, and the posse prepared to leave. Harris stood for a second watching, then, with a stifled cry of rage, rushed to the stable and emerged a few moments later on his horse. Taylor and Kitson were only seconds behind him. They caught up with the posse in the space of a quarter of a mile, and drew up alongside Appleby and his prisoner.

'We're ridin' in to Yavapai with yu,' Harris said, defiance in his voice.

Appleby shrugged, although he could not keep all of the venom from his voice as he replied, 'It ain't necessary.'

'Never said it was,' Jake told him. 'I just figgered if we was along Jim wouldn't take it into his head to do suthin' foolish, like mebbe makin' a run for it.'

He smiled as Appleby's head jerked and the lawman laid a burning gaze upon the prisoner. The old homesteader had made his meaning crystal clear, and none of the posse had missed the inference: Harris did not trust the Marshal or his posse out of sight. Green would hardly be the first prisoner to have been killed under the umbrella of *ley del fuego*, the old bounty-hunter's foolproof way of bringing in prisoners who were wanted dead or alive, and were easier to handle dead. Such prisoners were always 'shot trying to escape', and their brutal murder was tacitly accepted by the Law which paid the rewards for their bodies.

'Do as yu please,' snarled Appleby. 'I ain't no backshooter.'

'Never said yu was,' agreed Harris equably.

The posse moved on down the trail towards the town, leaving a cloud of sun-silvered dust hanging heavy in their wake.

CHAPTER TWENTY-ONE

ON the morning of the trial old Smithy, the stove-up puncher who kept the jail clean and acted as an unpaid jailer in return for a roof over his head and a few dollars for drinks, shuffled over and rattled a tin cup against the bars of Sudden's cell.

'Rise an' shine, Mr. Sudden,' he cackled. 'Yu gotta be up bright an' early. Wouldn't want to miss all the fun, would yu?' His rheumy eyes watered as he enjoyed his own humour. 'Want some cawfee?'

'If yu mean that dishwater I been drinkin', no thanks,' Sudden told him, smiling inwardly at the old man's enjoyment. Smithy had become more important these last few days than at any time in his life. Having the celebrated Sudden as his charge had made the old man garrulous, and he had spent the night reminiscing about his years on the Chisholm Trail.

'Yu reckon yu could loan me a razor?' Sudden asked the old man. 'Might as well look as little like a bum as possible.'

He gestured ruefully at the three-day stubble on his chin, and the creased clothes which were the result of his confinement. Jake Harris had been in to see him several times; he and his two neighbours were staying in town until the trial was over, and Sudden had done his best to reassure the old homesteader about his predicament.

'They tell me it's all goin' to be legal an' above board,' he had told his employer. 'Appleby's sent down to Tucson for a circuit judge.'

'He's been stirrin' things up a mite, too,' growled the old man angrily. 'Not to mention that loud-mouthed son o' Gunnison's. It'll go bad if they find yu guilty, Jim.'

'Hell, I ain't expectin' it,' Sudden had smiled, but in truth he was perturbed that the tenor of the town might be conducive to violence which would involve his friends. The shave made him feel much better, and he sat down to eat the bacon and beans Smithy had heated up. After he had finished he rolled a cigarette and leaned back against the wall of his cell.

'Yu shore don't act like a man might be hanged by sunset,' the old man observed.

'Ain't plannin' on it, ol'timer,' Sudden told him with a smile.

'They says yo're as guilty as hell.'

'No sign o' Gunnison's body yet, then?'

'Nary a one. Appleby's had men out in the Mesquites every day. Ol' Lafe Gunnison's just plain disappeared.'

'Yu know Gunnison well?' asked the captive.

'Know everyone in this town,' boasted Smithy. 'Been here a slew o' years. Worked for Tom Appleby's predecessor, afore he was killed.'

'When was that?' asked Sudden.

'Two year or more ago. Rock-slide caught him up in the Yavapais. He was a good man, George Rogers.'

'How come Appleby was made Marshal?'

'Don't recollect exackly,' Smithy said, scratching his stubbled chin. 'He arrove in town, applied for the job. Randy Gunnison spoke for him, as I recall. Knowed him in Santa Fé, or some such place. He had some references. Been a good Marshal. How come yo're askin' so many questions?'

'On'y way to get answers,' Sudden told him, grinning.

'I hope yu got a few for the trial,' Smithy retorted, his sly old face grim. 'Yo're shore goin' to need 'em, boy.'

* * *

By the time ten o'clock, the hour advertised for the opening of the trial, arrived the entire population of Yavapai and not a few strangers were crowded into Tyler's saloon. The milling spectators jostled each other for the best vantage points from which to see the trial, and the atmosphere was almost one of holiday. Jovial insults, curses, greetings were being tossed backwards and forward across the room as various denizens of the town recognised their cronies and hailed them. Against the wall at the back of the room the homesteaders arrayed themselves; absent were Philadelphia and Susan Harris, who had stayed with the boy because she could, as she put it, 'take better care of him than he could of himself'. The faces of Sudden's friends were glum. They had spent the preceding evening going over and over the accusations against their friend, without ever being able to suggest a suitable alternative to put to the Sheriff. Their knowledge of the involvement of Randy Gunnison and Jim Dancy in the thefts of Sabre beef was their only ace-in-the-hole, and they had, at Sudden's suggestion, refrained from playing that card until they were forced to. Now, they could only hope that the young puncher himself would convince the jurors that the case against him was too fragile and flimsy to support a verdict of guilty.

The jury were arrayed on chairs set in two rows at right-angles to the bar, in front of which was a table and two chairs for the prisoner and his captor. Behind the bar a raised platform had been placed, which made of the long bar a kind of judicial bench behind which Harvey Mattingley, the circuit judge, would sit. He was, so one patron of the saloon informed a neighbour, due this morning from Tucson. An open space in front of the prisoner's table had been left clear, presumably for anyone wishing to address or approach the bench, and at the side opposite the jury a witness-box consisting of a chair and an old reading lectern loaned by the Yavapai Valley Bank had been placed.

Shortly after half past nine a coach pulled to a halt in a cloud of dust outside the Marshal's office. The few passers-by remarked on the fact that the horses had been punishingly used, and conjectured upon the identity of the visitor. They waited to see a short, rather corpulent man descend from the coach. Dressed in a suit of dark broadcloth, trousers fitted neatly into the tops of shining boots, a narrow-brimmed black hat and a soft white shirt with black four-in-hand, he looked like a preacher or a gambler except for a certain air of authority in his bearing which set him apart from these professions. The passers-by hurried to Tyler's with the news that the judge had arrived as the short man went into Appleby's office.

The Marshal rose to meet his visitor, an oily smile upon his face.

'Yu'll be Judge Mattingley, I'm guessin',' he said. 'I'm Appleby, the Marshal.'

The visitor appeared not to see the proffered hand, and said, 'Judge Mattingley was detained, I'm afraid. I have come to take his place. My name is Bleke.'

Appleby's mouth fell open. This quiet little man with the shrewd grey eyes was an almost legendary figure. To have the Governor of Arizona come personally to superintend the trial was a surprise of such magnitude that Appleby was lost for words.

'Don't stand there with your mouth open, man,' snapped Bleke, with just a shade of irritation in his voice. 'Where does the hearing take place?'

Appleby took hold of himself. This could be turned to real advantage. If Bleke endorsed the verdict of the jury, and Appleby had taken certain steps to make that verdict a foregone conclusion, then Harris would be ruined and forced to leave the country. The hanging of the outlaw, Sudden, was incidental to Appleby's plans. His thin mouth curved in satisfaction at the thought, none the less.

'Right this way, Governor,' he fawned. 'We rigged up the saloon the best we could. They'll bring Sudden over as soon as yu give the word.'

Bleke nodded and accompanied the Marshal to Tyler's saloon. A hush fell on the audience as they entered, and Appleby nodded to Smithy to bring in the prisoner. Bleke took his seat behind the bar and surveyed the crowded room with cold eyes.

'My name is Bleke,' he told them, ignoring the hum of comment which his announcement caused. 'I will be conducting this hearing and I want it known at the outset that I will tolerate no rowdiness or disorder. Let me make it quite clear. I can live up to my name when I have to.' After a pause in which he let his double-meaning sink in, he turned to Appleby.

'Where is the prisoner?'

'He's right here, Guv'nor,' cackled old Smithy, leading in the tightly bound cowboy. Bleke's face tightened.

'Why is this man tied up?' he snapped.

'Why ... he's ... he's a wanted murderer, Governor,' stammered the Marshal.

'I understood he was accused of murder, not guilty of it,' Bleke rapped out. 'Or have you tried him already?'

Appleby shook his head dumbly, and Bleke gave the order to cut Sudden loose.

'Phew, he's an ol' tyrant, ain't he?' one spectator whispered to his neighbour. 'I wonder what's bitin' him?'

'Search me,' retorted the listener. 'Whatever it is, I bet he bit it first.' They returned their attention to Bleke, who was leaning now across the bar, addressing the prisoner.

'You are Sudden, the outlaw?'

'Men call me that, seh.'

'James Green is your real name?'

'It's the one I use,' was the reply.

'You understand that we are not interested in the fact that you are wanted in Texas, Mr. Green?' Sudden nodded, his eyes veiled. The Governor asked him who would conduct his defence.

'I reckon I'll do 'er myself, seh,' was the puncher's reply, at which Bleke nodded to the Marshal.

'We are ready, Marshal.'

Appleby stepped forward. 'It's my intention to show that the accused, James Green, alias Sudden, murdered——'

'Dispense with the icing, Marshal.' The cold voice of the Governor cut into Appleby's speech with an irritable intonation. Startled by the interruption Appleby turned to face Bleke.

'That's somewhat unconventional, Governor,' he protested.

'I'm inclined to be unconventional, Marshal,' was the

unsmiling reply. 'Get on with it.'

Appleby nodded, and motioned to Randy Gunnison to enter the witness-box.

'Tell the court what happened on the mornin' o' the day yore ol' ma—yore father disappeared.'

'Well ... my father had been getting more and more upset about the steady losses the Sabre had been suffering through rustling. He always thought that the nesters were behind it, but it was impossible to prove without starting a full-scale range war, and he did not want that. Hc told me that morning that he thought maybe if he talked to Jake Harris on a man-to-man basis they might get it settled.'

'Did he tell anyone else about this?'

'Not to my knowledge, no.'

'Anyone else see him leave the ranch?'

'Jim Dancy, our—my foreman, saw him go.'

Appleby turned to face the Governor. 'Dancy'll so state if yu wish, Governor.'

Bleke nodded. 'Proceed,' he said.

'What time o' day was it yore father left Sabre?'

'Just after breakfast. About seven, maybe seven-thirty.'

'Yu tried to persuade him not to go?'

'I told him he was mad to go up there alone. He said that if he took the men with him the nesters'd think it was a war party, and he didn't want any shooting.'

'What happened then?'

'You know all this,' protested Randy.

'Shore, I was there,' Appleby nodded. 'But the Governor here ain't heard the facts. Yu tell it just like it happened.'

'Well ... yu came in about ten o'clock. We were having coffee when Dancy came yelling in from the corral that my father's horse had come home with blood on the saddle.'

Appleby turned to face the bench. 'There was a lot o' blood on the saddle,' he told the Governor. 'I found pine needles caught in the hoss's shoes, so I knew he'd been up in the Mesquites. That's the only place yu can find needles that thick. We figgered something had happened, but we didn't know what. I sent Dancy to try to back track the old man, but it was no use, he couldn't find anythin'. I rode back into town for help.'

'Why did you do that rather than wait for the Sabre riders to come in off the range?' interposed Bleke.

'We figgered if Sabre blundered up into the Mesquites in force the same thing Gunnison had feared would happen. In addition it was gettin' dark. We didn't know where to start lookin'—that's a fairly big area up there.'

The Marshal nodded to Gunnison and then turned to his prisoner. 'Ask any questions yu want to,' he said. Sudden got slowly to his feet and walked across the space to the witness-box. He stopped with his narrowed eyes only a foot from Randy Gunnison's and shot out a question.

'With yore father dead, who owns the Sabre now?'

'I don't quite see ... I suppose I do.'

'How much would yu say Sabre was worth?'

Gunnison turned towards Bleke, appealing for his support.

'I don't see what this is about,' he remonstrated. Bleke's expression did not change.

'You will answer,' he told Gunnison.

'Oh, not that it matters,' sniffed Randy. 'About a hundred or a hundred and fifty thousand dollars. It would need an expert appraisal.'

'So yu'll be a rich man?' pursued Sudden.

'I don't follow you.'

'I'm suggestin' that mebbe yu had a motive for killin' Lafe Gunnison yoreself!'

Randolph Gunnison leapt to his feet. 'How dare you say that!' he screeched. 'How dare you!' Appleby was on his feet, too, protesting Sudden's tactics, while Governor Bleke pounded on the bar for order.

'Do you have any evidence to support such an accusation, Green?' barked Bleke. Sudden shook his head and returned to his seat, content to have planted a seed of doubt in the minds of those watching the proceedings.

A buzz of conversation arose as Appleby motioned Jim Dancy to the stand. It ceased abruptly at one rap of Bleke's mallet.

'Yu saw Lafe Gunnison leave the Sabre?' asked Appleby. Dancy nodded. 'Now tell us: did Randolph Gunnison leave the ranch at any time after his father had gone, or up to the time I arrived?'

Dancy shook his head. 'Nope. Not at all.'

'He couldn't've slipped out without yore seein' him?'

'Not possible,' Dancy said emphatically.

Appleby sat down, and Sudden again stood. This time, however, he remained behind the table.

'Did yu ever hear Wes Cameron mentioned by Lafe Gunnison?'

'Not so as I can recall,' Dancy said.

'Yu know Cameron killed two homesteaders in town, o' course.'

'I know it. An' I know what happened to Cameron because of it.'

Bleke's gavel again raped as Dancy's insult prompted a murmur from the spectators.

'Yu don't reckon Gunnison hired Cameron, then?' asked Green.

'I don't know,' Dancy said. 'He mighta done.'

Sudden wheeled to face Randy Gunnison, who had returned to his seat in the front row of the court.

'Yo're still on oath, Gunnison,' he snapped. 'Did yore ol' man hire Wes Cameron to kill them two men?'

'Certainly not!' came the emphatic denial. Sudden nodded grimly and motioned Jake Harris to come forward and take the stand.

'One question, Mr. Harris,' he told the homesteader. 'Did yu hire Wes Cameron to kill two o' yore friends?'

'By God, Jim, if any other man but yu had asked that I'd kill him, court or no court! The answer's no! No!'

Bleke leaned forward as the old homesteader rose from the chair.

'You were probably justifiably angry at the way in which the question was put, Mr. Harris. Nevertheless, I draw attention to your outburst only to point out that I will not tolerate another in this court.'

Appleby stepped forward.

'Just a minute, Jake, I got a question for yu.' He rocked on his heels, waiting a moment for the tension to grow before he asked, 'Did yu hire this Sudden feller knowin' his reputation?'

'I did. I reckon he's probably not guilty o' half the things they say he done.'

'Nevertheless, yu hired him. A known killer. I'll ask yu the question that Mr. Sudden forgot. Did yu hire him to kill Lafe Gunnison?'

This time Jake Harris had his temper firmly under control, although a vein throbbed in his forehead and the muscles of his neck bulged with the effort.

'Certainly not,' he managed.

'If he did, he isn't likely to admit it,' sneered Randy Gunnison.

Bleke rapped the bar. 'Another remark like that, my boy, and you'll do thirty days for contempt of court. Hold your tongue!'

Gunnison subsided, but Sudden knew that Jake's denial had been offset by the sly remark. He stood up and turned to Appleby.

'Would yu take the stand, Marshal?'

Appleby looked his surprise, but his confidence was high. Yo're on the run, Mr. Sudden, he gloated inwardly. He leaned back in the chair and faced his questioner.

'Yu already heard Gunnison there say he was shore his old man didn't hire Cameron. Yu heard Jake Harris swear on oath that he didn't either. If neither o' them hired Cameron, who did?'

'I ain't heard anyone say anything to show Cameron was hired at all,' Appleby said with a cold smile.

'Yu think he just rode in here by accident, picked a fight with Johnstone an' Newley, killed 'em for no reason?'

'He killed 'em in self-defence, far as I recall,' Appleby reminded him. 'So where does that leave yu?' His voice was gloating.

'The same place it leaves yu, actually,' Green said. His smile was cold and mirthless, and for a moment Appleby felt an icy finger of panic touch his spine.

'What yu drivin' at, Green?' he spat.

'Yu ain't answered the question yu asked everyone else, Marshal,' Sudden said reasonably. 'Where was yu when Gunnison was killed?'

Appleby's jaw dropped. Too late he saw the hole in his plan, the one false step which this smiling devil had seen from the start. His mind raced furiously as he tried to anticipate Green's questions and think simultaneously.

'Yu left the Harris place an' rode towards Sabre,' Sudden said inexorably. 'At the same time yu was leavin' the JH, Gunnison was leavin' the Sabre. Yu both took the same trail. *Yet yu didn't see him*. How come, Marshal?'

Appleby shrugged, maintaining an outward air of calmness which he hoped concealed his desperation.

'Search me,' he said. 'Mebbe he didn't use the trail. Mebbe he seen me an' thought I was one o' the homesteaders, an' dodged me.'

'Funny,' Sudden snapped. 'Yu arrest me claimin' I ran into Gunnison an' bumped him off—an' he don't even try to sidestep me—yet yu claim he dodges off the trail to avoid a man he knows well. Does that sound likely?'

A constant murmur of speculation washed around the room as the spectators, for the first time, realised that Appleby was in a position from which he could not extricate himself. Somehow the dark-haired cowboy had turned the tables; now it was the Marshal who was on trial, not Sudden.

'I'm goin' to repeat somethin' yu said to me,' Sudden told him, advancing to place himself squarely in front of the lawman. 'I got a man who had the time, the opportunity, an' the reason.'

Appleby's eyes swept the courtroom wildly, seeking support from the faces of the spectators. None could he see; every face was set, and they awaited Sudden's next words with tense anticipation. It was Appleby who spoke first, however, biting back the terror that threatened to rise in his throat.

'Yo're out o' yore mind,' he croaked. 'Why would I want to kill Lafe Gunnison?'

Sudden turned to the Governor. 'I got a surprise witness, seh.' He turned and pointed with his chin to where Terry Kitson was shepherding in an old man with greying hair and a silvery beard. Randy Gunnison half rose in his chair, a strangled sound coming from his throat. Appleby sat stock still, only his eyes moving.

Speculation about the old man's identity created a buzz of talk in the room, but silence fell immediately Sudden started to speak.

'Thisyere is Shorty Willis,' he told Bleke. 'Tell us yore story, Shorty.'

The old man nodded, and in a dry, cracked voice recounted the details which Sudden had heard, those many nights ago, in the little shack up in the mountains. There was dead silence as the spectators listened to the old man's unvarnished account of how he had been fooled into looking after the Sabre cattle, and of the involvement of Randy Gunnison and his foreman. There were harsh murmurs from some of the men watching, for treachery of this sort was outside even their easy-going set of moral rules. When the old man had finished speaking Sudden whirled to face Randolph Gunnison. 'What have yu got to say, Gunnison?'

Randy Gunnison's mouth opened but no sound came out. He tried to say something, but before he could utter the words another voice cut harshly in. It was the deep voice of Jim Dancy, and every word was a whiplash of contempt.

'That damned ol' desert-rat!' he laughed. 'He used to herd a few head for us up in the hills. I fired him about ten months ago when I found he was sellin' beef to anyone who'd buy it! I would'a' strung him up, 'ceptin' for the fact he's half crazy. Anyone takes his word for anythin's got to be more'n half loco hisself!'

Shorty Willis looked stunned as Dancy hurled these words into the silent room, stilling instantly the murmurs which, a moment before, had been directed against him and the son of Sabre's owner. Sudden muttered an oath beneath his breath. If Dancy had stayed silent a moment longer, Gunnison might have broken. Now, the man's colour was back, and he sat once more erect in his chair, his confidence bolstered by Dancy's well-timed lies.

Bleke leaned forward to speak to Shorty. 'Can you prove any of what you say?' he asked.

Shorty shook his head. 'It's my word agin his,' he muttered. 'I can't prove none of it. But them cattle is in that canyon, an' Jim Dancy brung 'em up there!'

All eyes turned again to the burly Sabre foreman, but his face was wreathed in a contemptuous sneer.

'They's no cattle in the Yavapais belongin' to Sabre!' he stated flatly, and with sinking hearts Sudden's friends realised that Dancy's obvious confidence indicated that he had made sure the cattle were no longer in the canyon.

'Hold yore hosses a moment, Dancy!' Sudden's voice was clarion clear, and halted the Sabre man in his tracks as he swaggered back to his seat, amid the congratulations of his hangers-on.

Dancy turned, a frown appearing on his face. 'What now?' he growled. 'Yu goin' to make some more wild claims?'

'Wait an' see,' Sudden advised him. He turned to face the jury. 'A while back,' he told them, 'Susan Harris an' Philadelphia, the kid workin' on the Harris place, was shot at from ambush.' An astonished murmur greeted this news; many of those present had not heard of this event. 'Philadelphia an' me tracked the bushwhacker as far as the Yavapai, where he crossed. It looked like he'd ridden to the Sabre, so we rode over an' talked to Lafe Gunnison about it.'

'An' got sent off with a flea in yore ear!' said Dancy scornfully, to the accompaniment of laughter from some of the hearers, who could imagine old Lafe Gunnison's reaction to the suggestion that the puncher was making.

'Somethin' happened yu don't know about, Dancy,' continued Sudden. 'When we left the ranch, I doubled back an' took a look in yore stables. I found a hoss that had been ridden hard, with sign on him that showed he'd been acrost the Yavapai. The jasper we'd trailed hadn't bothered to cover his sign much. Anyway, I marked that hoss so I'd know him again.'

Dancy looked startled for a moment, then his bravado returned. 'So what?' he said.

Sudden turned to a bystander. 'Would yu take a gander at Dancy's sorrel outside? See if yu can find a hair-brand o' my initials under the saddle—"JG", it oughta be right easy to find.'

The man hastened to do Sudden's bidding, while Dancy stood glaring at the puncher. His mind seethed as the whole room waited in silence for the verdict. It came like a thunderclap when the man at the door shouted in, 'The hoss is branded just like this feller sez!'

There was immediate commotion in the courtroom,

which lapsed into reluctant silence as Bleke pounded insistently with the hammer. The Governor turned towards Dancy.

'Do you have any comment, Dancy?' he queried, iron in his voice.

'Hell, Governor,' Dancy said querulously, 'I ain't denyin' my hoss could be carryin' this jasper's brand. We on'y got his word for it that he done it when he said he done it.'

'When else could I have done it, Dancy?' Sudden asked relentlessly.

'Makes no never mind when yu done it!' snapped the foreman of the Sabre. 'It shore don't prove I bushwhacked them kids up in the Mesquites!'

'We trailed a bushwhacker to the Yavapai, an' figgered he'd come from Sabre. We find yore hoss hard used, with sign he'd been across the river. An' yu deny yu know anythin' about it?' There was deep scorn in Sudden's voice which found an echo in the babble of speculation his words loosed among the watchers.

'I'll tell yu all I know,' Dancy rasped. 'But it won't do yu no good, mister. Yo're tryin' to throw sand in people's eyes by takin' their attention off the fac' that yu killed Lafe Gunnison! Well, the hell with yu, Mr. Sudden! I wondered whether someone had been monkeyin' around when I found one o' my men buffaloed in the stables a few hours after yu'd left Sabre. But nothin' was stolen, an' the man claimed he'd seen nothin', so I let it ride. Now yu tell me yu marked my hoss, an' expect these people to believe that it proves I took a shot at yore frien's. Yo're loco!' He hurled the last two words at Sudden with undisguised venom, and the puncher saw the answering flash of triumph appear in Appleby's eyes. He shook his head. Once again evidence of complicity had been negated by what amounted to brazen defiance. He could not prove that Dancy had been the ambusher, and Dancy knew it. At this juncture the Marshal rose to his feet.

'Governor, this play-actin's gone on long enough! This Sudden feller's wastin' time tryin' to throw up enough dust to fog the minds o' thisyere court. But every bit o' so-called evidence he trots out is as phoney as a three-dollar bill! I'm sayin' we orta get on with what we come here for—to try a killer!'

There were several shouts of 'Attaboy, Tom!' and 'That's tellin' him, Marshal!' from the back of the saloon at this speech, and Sudden realised that so far he had done nothing to weaken the solid foundation which Appleby and his tools had built in this town. The uproar was stilled by Bleke, whose ice-cold voice silenced the angry cries within seconds.

'Marshal, I think it fairly well established that on the face of the evidence either Green or yourself had the opportunity to kill Lafe Gunnison,' rapped the Governor. 'I do not appreciate your attempts at rabble-rousing. Don't make the mistake of trying it again in front of me!' He rapped the bar again for silence. 'Is there any further evidence against this man you wish to present?'

Appleby shook his head sullenly. He took three steps and faced Sudden, his face contorted.

'Well, Mr. Sudden,' he hissed. 'I ain't got yu, but yu ain't got me. Yu've accused me o' killin' Lafe Gunnison when every man in this town knows I've done my best to keep things peaceful here for two years. Yu've made other claims which ain't done anythin' except make yore standin' in this town worse. Yu ain't out o' the woods yet, Sudden! I'm still aimin' to find Lafe Gunnison's killer, an' I'm bettin' on it bein' yu!'

An angry sound rose from the massed spectators. Appleby's words had cleverly played upon their loyalty, for among the townspeople he had a reputation for square dealing that had always been to their liking.

'Yu lose yore bet, Appleby!' boomed a voice from the back of the room. The Marshal whirled to face the direction from which the voice had come, his hand flying to the gun at his side. His hand closed on empty air, and he turned to see Sudden holding the weapon levelled at his chest.

'Seen a ghost, Marshal?' gritted Sudden. Indeed, Appleby's face was ghastly enough to have convinced any onlooker that such was the case, and in truth the man was shaken by the sight which caused every man in the room to rise to his feet.

'My Gawd, it's Lafe Gunnison!' shouted one spectator, unable to repress his astonishment any longer.

'Yeah,' said another. 'What's left o' him.'

The old rancher looked like a man at death's door as he limped down the aisle between the chairs. Supporting his huge bulk by means of one of his arms over their shoulders were Susan Harris and Philadelphia, his face slightly grey under his tan. Gunnison's huge frame was wasted, and his formerly iron-grey hair had turned completely white. His face was marked by bruises and abrasions, and etched deep into his expression were the lines of pain and suffering. He lurched into the open space in front of the bench, spurning further help from Philadelphia and Susan, and came to a stop before his trembling son, who cowered before his father's accusing finger.

'There's yore killer: my own son!'

A cry of rage arose from the spectators, who completely ignored the insistent pounding of Bleke's gavel as they grabbed Randy Gunnison with none-too-gentle hands and stripped him of his hideaway gun, two men on each arm holding him prisoner as immutably as if he were chained to rock.

'Yes, my own son tried to kill me. Damn near succeeded, too! He must have thought I was cashed, shore. Whoever tossed me in that dry wash up in the Mesquites didn't even look to see if I was dead. I woke up with buzzards flapping around me. Laid there all day in the open. Finally, I managed to crawl to water. I must'a' passed out. I crawled a lot. All I knowed was it was downhill. Next thing I knew I was in a bed in the Harris place, with these two youngsters tendin' my wounds. When I regained consciousness they told me what had happened.' A dry cough racked his frame, and fresh redness stained the bandages around his chest. 'It . . . it's a lot worse than it looks,' he managed, trying to smile. He turned to his son, pain in every line of his face. 'I know yu never loved me,' he gasped. 'But why did yu try to kill me?'

Randolph Gunnison tried to wrench away from his captors, tried insanely to escape the accusation in his father's staring eyes. His captors held him immovably.

Spittle formed at the corners of his mouth, and his eyes rolled madly. 'I had to!' he screamed 'I had to! You kept asking and asking how I knew you hadn't hired Cameron. I was scared you'd guess it was Appleby....'

'Shut up, yu damned fool!' the Marshal roared in an agonised voice. 'Shut yore stupid mouth!'

'Take a mite o' your own advice, Marshal,' a cold voice warned him, and the lawman subsided as Sudden gestured minutely with the gun.

'He's been holding me to ransom ever since he came here!' Randy Gunnison was raving. 'I got into trouble in Santa Fe ... cards. A woman. There was a shooting ... I ... ran.... He followed me. Told me he could get me hung ... had to do what he said. He said ... if I did ... he'd make me rich'

'Rich?' coughed Gunnison. 'How did he aim to make yu richer than I could?' He reeled slightly, as though about to fall, and Sudden, thrusting the gun into the hands of a bystander with terse instructions to shoot Appleby if he moved an eyebrow, moved to support the old man. He lowered him gently to a chair, while Randy Gunnison continued to speak as though some trigger had been tripped in his mind and nothing could stop the flow of words.

'He knew about ... loot from robberies ... the Jefferson gang ... all hidden under a cabin, up in the ... Mesquites.... Two hundred thousand dollars. Under one of the nester's shacks.'

'So he had to clear the nesters out afore he could look for the money,' Sudden prompted the younger Gunnison.

A cackling laugh made him turn his head. Weak though he was, the old man was chortling in amusement.

'He believed that ol' fairy-tale?' He coughed, pain wracking his face. 'Hell, boy, there ain't no money up there! Never was.'

Appleby made as if to step forward, and immediately heavy hands restrained him forcefully. He writhed in the grasp of his captors and spat, 'Yo're lyin'! I know there's money up there!' He stopped, a crafty look crossing his face.

Sudden turned to face him. 'Yu were sayin' . . .?' he prompted.

'I'll see yu in hell,' cursed the Marshal.

'More'n likely,' agreed Sudden equably. 'Yo're right, Marshal. There was money up there. It was under Reb Johnstone's shack, and the total amount was . . . how much was it, Mr. Granger?'

'Two hundred and twenty three thousand, six hundred and forty dollars, sir,' announced the banker, enjoying the gasps of astonishment that the figures caused. Not a few of the men in the saloon looked at the struggling Appleby with sympathy for the first time since Gunnison had made his astounding entrance. The banker handed Sudden a large satchel, which the cowboy took across to Appleby.

'This has been in the bank since the day yu killed Cameron,' he said. 'This is what yu lied for an' murdered for, Marshal.' He emptied the satchel on the floor. Men craned their necks, jostled and shoved to catch a glimpse of the cascade of paper which Sudden emptied at Appleby's feet.

'Take a look at it!' Sudden's voice was a harsh command, and he snatched up a fistful of the money and thrust it under Appleby's nose. 'Take a good look, Appleby. Do yu know what the Jefferson boys stole? They robbed a train loaded with Confederate money that was being taken to Washington to be burned. Two hundred and twenty three thousand dollars—an' not worth the paper they're printed on.

'No . . .' Appleby's face was grey. 'No. Yo're lyin', yo're lyin', yo're lyin'!' His voice was a thin scream.

Randolph Gunnison, too, had been stricken by the revelation. He slumped now in the arms of the men who held him, weeping like a child. An astonished clatter of conversation filled the courtroom. Jake Harris pushed forward to ask his employee a question.

'Shucks, that was easy, seh,' Green told him. 'I just checked the land office maps for '66, which was when they caught the Jefferson boys. They only showed one cabin up in the Mesquites. Location was nigh on the same as Johnsone's. After that, it was only a matter o' diggin' it up.'

Now it was Lafe Gunnison's turn to speak. He got slowly to his feet and approached the bar, behind which Governor Bleke sat, his grey eyes not missing a movement in the room.

'Yo're Bleke,' Gunnison said softly.

'Yes, Gunnison. I'm Bleke.'

'It took yu long enough to get up here.'

Bleke smiled. 'Oh, no,' he told the old rancher. 'I've been here some considerable time. Not in person, of course. But when I got your first letter I sent my special deputy.'

Appleby overheard this exchange and looked from Bleke to Gunnison in utter confusion.

'He wrote to yu . . . about the Yavapai valley?'

Blede nodded. 'You were nothing like as subtle as you seem to think you were, Appleby. Green spotted you very quickly.'

'Green?' cried the lawman hoarsely. 'What's he got to do with it?'

'Everything,' Bleke told him, his voice cutting. 'Green is my special deputy. He has been acting on my orders throughout.'

Jake Harris stepped forward, his eyes shining and his hand out-thrust. 'I never thought I'd live to see the day I'd want to shake yore hand, Gunnison, but by God! I aim to do her now! If yu wrote to Governor Bleke askin' for help, that's all the proof I need that we can get along in the future.'

The two men shook hands warmly as a sullen rumble of thunder rattled the windows lightly and the sunlight outside turned a faintly darker shade of amber.

'Storm buildin' up in the Yavapais,' muttered Shorty Willis.

'It's the time o' year for them,' another oldtimer agreed.

Meanwhile, Bleke was beckoning to Gunnison and Sudden. His words stilled the hum of conversation which had arisen. 'There is one final point to be cleared up, gentlemen. Who was behind all these raids on the property of the homesteaders?'

'Well, Appleby was the brains, o' course,' Sudden said. 'But his orders was carried out by——'

'Stand damn still, every last one o' yu!' The command came from the grimly compressed lips of Jim Dancy, who had, as Sudden had started to indict him, leaped backwards towards the door of the saloon, clear of the clustered watchers of the drama in the court. A wicked sawn-off shotgun lay across his forearm, cocked and murderous.

'Don't nobody even blink,' he warned the silent crowd, 'or I'll spread this crowd around some.' He moved forward two steps and those nearest to him shrank backwards, away from the gaping muzzles of the shotgun. 'Clear a way, damn yore eyes!' grated the Sabre foreman. 'Yu'—he gestured with the gun towards Appleby's captors—'turn him loose!' The men holding the Marshal's arms complied hastily, and Appleby scuttled around until he was beside his companion in crime, dragging Susan Harris back with him, protecting his body with hers. He lifted a six-shooter from the holster of the nearest spectator, his face lit with a hellion's smile. Sudden, unarmed, watched helplessly as Randy Gunnison wailed plaintively, 'Dancy! What about me?'

'Stay an' hang, yu spineless jessy!' rasped Dancy.

Appleby was close to the door, gun cocked. His teeth shone whitely as he smiled wolfishly behind Dancy. 'One last thing,' he hissed. 'For yu, Sudden!' He raised the gun and fired, all in one movement, but the shot was hasty. Sudden felt the cold breath of the bullet on his temple, heard a grasping groan behind him from Randy Gunnison. The son of the Sabre owner slumped to the floor, blood pumping from a wound near his heart.

Appleby had not waited to see the result of his shot; he was already through the door, dragging the struggling Susan Harris along with him. The batwings swung inwards as Dancy backed towards them and caught the burly Sabre foreman on his shoulder, upsetting his balance for a fraction of a second. In that moment young Philadelphia moved, his gun belched flame. The bullet spun Dancy backwards out through the doors, the shotgun pellets blasting harmlessly into the ceiling. Dancy fell dead in the street outside as Sudden, scooping his gunbelt out of the old jailer's unresisting hands, dashed into the open in time to see Appleby thundering out of town towards the north, the girl slung half-conscious across his saddle in front of him. Men spewed out of the saloon, and one or two were about to fire after the fleeing lawman until Jake Harris stopped them with a sharp word; even if they were lucky enough to hit the fast-disappearing figure of Appleby, there was too much danger that Susan might also be hurt. Sudden was already in the saddle of the first horse he had found at the hitching-rail, and by the time others had followed his example he was out of the environs of the town and heading in pursuit of the fugitive lawman.

Over the prairies an evil yellow murk had descended. The Yavapais were already disappearing into slate-coloured cloud, and lightning flickered once or twice.

'Goin' to be a real one when she comes,' muttered Sudden, his eyes intent upon the dot on the open plain ahead which was Appleby. He cast a quick glance behind him. The rest of the pursuers were strung out in an uneven line, about two hundred yards to the rear. Off to his right he saw a lone horseman thundering eastwards, heading for the low hills lining the horizon, and wondered vaguely who it was. The first heavy spots of rain dashed against his face as he spurred the animal beneath him to ever greater speed. Slowly he drew nearer to his prey, pounding now along the trail towards the Mesquites.

'Runnin' scared an' runnin' blind,' was Sudden's first thought, but then he realised that such was not the case at all. Appleby was heading for the Badlands, the rough, flint-covered edging to the desert. 'If he gets in there I'll lose him shore,' he told himself, renewing his efforts to coax even more speed from the horse, wishing as he did so that he had had time to find Nigger, who would have run down with ease the double-laden animal Appleby was riding. Crooning to the horse, Sudden peered ahead into the murk. He was gaining on Appleby. The lawman was now only about five hundred yards ahead, and veering eastwards off the trail towards the Badlands. The rain was becoming heavier now; it splattered wickedly into Green's eyes as he raced on.

'Ain't any better for him,' he consoled himself. 'Worse, probably . . . tryin' to cope with the girl as well.'

Off to the left now he could just distinguish a dark mass which he realised must be the wooden bridge across Borracho Creek. A quick glance over his shoulder revealed no sign of the rest of the pursuers. He smiled grimly to himself.

'He's got to slow down for Borracho Creek,' he thought. 'Them crick sides are too steep to ride down at that speed.' Then, 'My Gawd!'

This last expletive was occasioned as Appleby, without slacking his horse's speed one iota, hit the edge of Borracho Creek and went over. The horse tried frantically to keep its balance as its forefeet slid on the steep creek banks, the clay giving no purchase. With the double load, however, the animal could not stay upright, and with a scream that echoed shrilly across the now-silent prairie the horse fell forward, throwing its rider and his prisoner over its head. Susan Harris lay where she had fallen, stunned; but Appleby by some miracle was unhurt, and scrambled to the shelter of some large rocks scattered along the creek bed.

Pulling his mount to a sliding stop, Sudden threw himself to the ground as Appleby's shots whined about his head. Slowly the puncher edged forward. Risking a quick glance around the side of the rock behind which he was crouched, he was just in time to discern, through the veil of rain, Appleby's form scuttling up the creek towards another jumble of rocks. He threw a hasty shot at the fugitive, and edged forward. Below him he could see Susan Harris; she was stirring slightly as the drumming rain revived her. Sudden was wet through now, and he chanced a quick dash forward, hoping that the bad light and the rain would spoil Appleby's aim. Several shots whined about him ineffectually as he slithered behind another rock, just at the edge of the creek bed. The rain had turned into a torrent now, and thunder crashed incessantly above them. From the south another thunder-roll, different in intensity and tone, caught his attention momentarily, but he dismissed the distraction as he concentrated upon his inch-by-inch forward progress. He slithered over the edge of the creek bed. Totally exposed now to Appleby's shots, he rolled over on to his left side, trying to grasp the damp clay, to get enough purchase to throw a shot at Appleby if the lawman showed himself. His slide stopped when his questing hand clutched a sparse tuft of grama grass, and he found himself within a few feet of Susan Harris.

'Yu all right, ma'am?' he asked.

'Yes ... I think so. Is .. is he ...?'

'No, he ain't. I lost sight o' him. I think he's behind those rocks over there. Can yu move?'

'I'll try,' she said gamely. But when she moved her leg she paled, her face twisted with pain. 'It's my ankle,' she moaned. 'I think I've twisted it.'

Green reached his left hand for her, digging his heels into the clay bank for purchase. It was no good. Her dead weight was too much for him to move one-handed. He holstered his revolver and pulled the girl towards him, hearing as he did so that same curious thunder that he had heard before, but louder now, and nearer. In that same moment Tom Appleby slid into sight over the edge of the creek bed, his gun cocked and aimed at Sudden's heart.

'Well, well,' he jeered, panting. 'Rescuin' damsels in distress seems to be yore speciality, Sudden. I'll see it's carved on yore tombstone.' So saying, he raised the six-shooter, his face distorted with hatred, while Sudden, taking one last desperate gamble, rolled sideways away from the expected shot, his mud-covered hand flashing for the holstered gun at his side. Before he had drawn properly a shot thundered out, and Appleby's leg buckled under him. The shot which was to have killed Sudden whined off into the darkness, and Sudden's shot, fired as he lay on his back supporting the dead weight of the girl, took the lawman high in the chest, sending him rearing upwards, toppling backwards, falling against the top level of the creek bed and sliding downwards at an angle on the rainslick clay, to slump huddled in a heap at the bottom. For a moment Sudden thought he heard the man cursing him, but at that instant Philadelphia's head appeared above him, and the boy yelled, 'Jim! Jim! Get up here! *Get up! Run for it!*' The thunder Sudden had heard before was now a roar, and it seemed to mount to monstrous proportions even as he heard it. A cold chill touched Sudden as he realised what it was.

Flash flood!

The heavy rains had gathered in the low foothills until they were rivulets, then streams, then together had channelled into this twisting creek bed to form a roaring, raging monster of a river. He remembered Jake Harris's words to Philadelphia: 'Keep a good fifty yards away if it looks like rain in the hills!' Philadelphia's extended hand helped him the last few feet up the side of the creek bed, and he scrambled to his feet, lifting the girl as if she weighed no more than a baby, and ran flat out up the slope and across the level prairie to where he had left the horse, paced by the hobbling Philadelphia. Behind them the thunder grew to incredible proportions and through the murk they could see vaguely a churning torrent of dark brown water sweeping along the creek bed towards the Yavapai. They lay in the pouring rain, their lungs labouring, as the water smashed down past them, hurling on its crest huge stones and uprooted trees, smashing them to gravel and kindling, roaring over the edges of the creek bed, lapping only a few yards from where the two men and the girl lay. In a few seconds a raging torrent filled the entire creek bed, and only the sound of the hissing rain and a growl of far-off thunder could be heard. Sudden looked bleakly at his companion, who stood with his arm about the shoulders of the sobbing Susan Harris.

'I guess he probably never knew what hit him, huh, Jim?' said Philadelphia.

Sudden nodded, a terrible weariness descending upon him. 'I guess not,' he said, glad that the boy had not heard Appleby's final, terrible scream.

Two minutes later the townspeople found them.

CHAPTER TWENTY-TWO

A WEEK had passed, and much had happened. Governor Bleke had returned to Tucson, and already the new Marshal he had appointed was on his way to Yavapai.

A crowd of irate townsfolk, led by Gunnison's crew from the Sabre, had stormed into Riverton and, after a running chase, captured Rance Fontaine. The fat man, Vince, had died defiantly, guns blazing to the last, cut down by a hail of bullets from the posse. Fontaine had been hung from the nearest tree. Jim Dancy had been buried on Boot Hill alongside his partner in crime, Randy Gunnison. The body of the villainous Marshal of Yavapai had never been found.

Old Lafe Gunnison, now rapidly recovering from his wound, had sent one of his riders across to the Mesquites with a note asking Sudden and Philadelphia to ride across to see him. The Sabre rider, whose name was Higgins, answered one of Sudden's questions with a grin.

'Jack Mado? I'd figger he was halfway to Montana by now. He must'a' been in Tyler's when Dancy made his play, an' sneaked out while the goin' was good.'

'At that, he got a better break than he deserved!' growled Jake Harris.

'He was just a tool,' Sudden told him. 'I misdoubt he knowed much about what was goin' on. He probably just done what Randy tol' him, 'thout worryin' much about the meanin' o' what he was doin'.'

Sudden and Philadelphia saddled up and accompanied Higgins back to the Sabre, where they were welcomed by the burly old rancher, now looking considerably more like the man they had met here those many days past. Sudden remarked upon this fact with a grin, and Gunnison nodded.

'Feelin' better, too,' he said. 'Like havin' a poison' arrer pulled outa yore hide. Can't do nothin' but good.'

As they entered the house the cook bustled in with coffee, a sly grin on his face.

'Never thought I'd see the day we was feedin' them damn' nesters, boss,' he told Gunnison.

'Yu better get used to it,' the rancher told him. 'I'm thinkin' we'll be doin' it a lot more.'

After a while the rancher turned to Sudden.

'I'm interested to know how yu finally cottoned on to Appleby's scheme, Jim,' he said. 'I had him figgered as straight.'

'So did I, at first,' Sudden replied. 'I reckon yu could

say it was process of elimination what done it.'

'How so?' queried Gunnison.

'Well, seh, it allus seemed mighty strange to me that a man who owned the Sabre'd be small-minded enough to want the homesteaders off their land—accordin' to the stories Appleby told Harris—one minnit an' then write to the Governor askin' him to send someone to investigate things the next.'

'I tell yu, writin' them letters was the best thing I ever done,' Gunnison told the two men.

'O' course, yu mighta been foxy enough to write to Bleke in order to throw suspicion off yoreself,' smiled Sudden. 'However, there was any number o' men in Tucson who was willing to swear that Lafe Gunnison was straight as a die, an' about as subtle as a stampede. After I talked with yu I agreed with them. Overhearin' Dancy in yore stables gave me the clue I needed that somethin' was happenin' on Sabre without yore knowin'.'

'An' yu knowed Harris was straight?' asked Gunnison.

'I knew nothin' to start off with,' Sudden replied. 'But I didn't have to live on the JH long to know Jake had no part in stealin' yore beef. So—the process of elimination. There wasn't many other candidates. Trouble was tryin' to prove it. If Randy had really killed yu—if he hadn't panicked in the courtroom—Appleby'd probably be a free man today.'

'A smilin' damned villain,' roared Gunnison, 'who turned a son agin his own father for a measley sack o' dollars!'

'Yu gotta remember, seh,' Sudden put in slyly, 'that Appleby didn't know the money was worthless. An' he stood to win irregardless. The way he planned it, somebody was goin' to be forced out o' the valley. If yu went to war agin Harris, one o' yu jugheads would'a' been killed. If Harris was forced out, Appleby would'a' filed on his land. If yu was killed, he had the Sabre. I'm guessin' Randy was next on Appleby's list for killin', anyway.'

'He had it tied up pretty neat,' commented Philadelphia.

'That's for shore,' agreed Sudden. 'He on'y made one mistake: tryin' to pin yore death on me, 'thout thinkin' about it long enough. I'm guessin' he was stampeded some—he shore didn't plan on Randy tryin' to kill yu.'

'That—that ingrate!' choked Gunnison. 'To think my own son . . .' Words failed him, and he struggled for a moment with his own private grief. After a moment he straightened, and bent his attention on Philadelphia.

'There's somethin' else I been meaning to talk to yu about,' he said. 'When yu was lookin' after me on Harris's place . . . it kept comin' to me . . . somethin' I thought when I first seen yu, boy. I ast Susan Harris about yu. She told me what yu'd told her about yoreself.'

Philadelphia looked at the rancher in bewilderment.

'I don't foller yore drift, seh,' he told Gunnison.

'Yu will in a minnit,' Gunnison smiled. 'Yore name's Henry Sloane, I'm told. How come yu got that name "Philadelphia"?'

'Shucks, that's easy, seh,' interposed Sudden. 'I gave him that monicker when he told us where he come from.'

Gunnison looked hard at the youngster.

'Yu recall yore mother's name, boy?'

'Of course,' Philadelphia said, nettled. 'It was——'

'Diane—right?' Gunnison's face was wreathed in a self-satisfied smile.

Philadelphia nodded. 'But how . . .?' he began.

'How do I know? I know more than that, boy. Let me tell yu what I know. Yore mother's name was Diane; her maiden name was Diane Lloyd Sloane. She married a good-for-nothin' puncher, an' they settled down to raise a family on a small spread down near Prescott. After her second son was born she was mighty ill. She went back East to recuperate, an' her family convinced her it would be a damn foolish thing to go back to the life that had near killed her. They got their family doctor to tell her so; and she stayed, keepin' her son with her. She'd left her eldest boy with her husband.'

Philadelphia's eyes were wide, his mouth hung slack at these details about his own life that he had never known.

'How . . . how do yu know all this?' he whispered.

'Hell, boy, it oughta be easy to figger. Diane Sloane was my wife! She was yore mother! When her family talked her into stayin' with them she went back to usin' her maiden name. Yu was brought up thinkin' it was the on'y one yu had. But it ain't. Yore name is Henry Gunnison—my youngest son—Hank!'

There were tears in the old rancher's eyes, and Philadelphia stood trembling at the revelations he had just heard, his own eyes swimming. He looked at Sudden with a plea in his expression and, nodding, the puncher rose and left the two of them alone. Outside he rolled a cigarette and blew smoke at the stars.

'If that don't beat all,' he told himself. 'Well, I reckon that takes care o' the kid's future. An' Sue Harris's, too, or I miss my bet.' He flicked the butt of the cigarette into the yard, where it spun in a shower of sparks against the dark earth. Sudden straightened and turned to go in once again. There was a trace of sadness in his face, and for a moment, with all the hard lines erased from his expression, he looked curiously young and lost.

Inside the ranchhouse he found Gunnison and his new-found son glaring at each other like sworn enemies. He pushed back his stetson with a thumb, eyeing them in consternation.

'Hey!' he protested. 'What happened to the fam'ly gatherin'?'

'I just told him that no son o' mine is marryin' any nester's spawn,' rasped Lafe Gunnison. 'I've had my bellyfull o' Harris an' his breed. I didn't find my son to lose him to some dirt-farmer's daughter!'

Philadelphia glared at the old man, his face white and set.

'If yu was a well man I'd thrash yu for them words!' he ground out. 'I aim to marry her if she'll have me. An' to hell with yu an' yore lousy ranch!'

'Then marry her an' be damned! I'll see yu don't get a cent o' my money!' Gunnison flung at the youngster.

'Keep it!' Henry said through clenched teeth. 'Keep yore ranch an' yore money! I got along fine without yu all these years—I guess I'll manage to survive another few without yore help!'

Red with suppressed rage, he wheeled and pushed past Sudden towards the door, only to be stopped in mid-stride by the sound of Lafe Gunnison's hearty bellow of laughter. He turned in amazement to face the old man, surprise in every line of his features.

'Jest wanted to be shore yu knowed yore mind, boy!' chortled Gunnison. 'Come here an' sit yoreself down. Damme, I'd be right proud to have Jake Harris's girl as a daughter-in-law.'

'Yu—yu ol' pirut!' managed Henry. 'Yu win: I buy the drinks next time we hit Yavapai!' He turned to his friend, who had smilingly watched the exchange between the two. 'Jim, yu reckon I can train this ol' mustang over, an' housebreak him?'

Sudden shook his head. 'Mighty hard row to hoe,' he told the boy, smiling.

'What I figgered,' Henry said. 'Mebbe my ... my Dad'll second my idea I got.'

'Go ahead, boy,' rumbled Gunnison. 'Yo're goin' to be runnin' Sabre soon enough. Now's as good a time as any to get started.'

He stood up, and placed his burly arm around his son's shoulder.

'We'd be mighty glad if yu could stay on here as ramrod, Jim,' Henry said. 'I ain't up to it, yet, an' we're goin' to need someone to run things.'

'I got a hunch Henry's goin' to be busy for a while,' smiled his father mischievously. 'What d'yu say, Jim?'

'It's a mighty temptin' offer, seh,' replied Sudden, 'but I got to turn her down. I'll be movin' on, I reckon.'

'Yu ain't stayin'?' blurted Henry, dismay in his voice.

'It's somethin' I got to do, Philadelphia,' Sudden told him. 'I got to find a couple o' men. Mebbe yu've heard o' them, seh? Names are Webb an' Peterson.' He directed his question at the rancher.

Gunnison shook his head. 'Can't say I ever heard the names,' he admitted. 'What yu want 'em for?'

'We got some unfinished business together,' was all Sudden would say. They were to recall his words when, some years later, the news filtered into the Yavapai valley of how he had found the men he was seeking.* His young face was cold and hard as he spoke.

Sudden thrust out his hand, and Gunnison took it.

'I'm wishin' yu success,' the puncher told him. 'Yu don't need wishin' happiness.' He turned and left before the old rancher could find the words he wanted to say.

* Related in *The Range Robbers* (Corgi Books).

Henry followed his friend out on the porch. He could see Nigger patiently awaiting his master at the hitching-rail. Sudden turned to face his young protégé.

'Philadelphia, I got one more favour to ask yu,' he said slowly.

The boy nodded eagerly. 'Shore, Jim—anythin'.'

'Yu say goodbye to Harris and the rest o' them for me. I never was much of a hand at it.' His voice was gruff as they clasped hands.

'Any time yu feel like it, yu come back here,' Henry said, awkwardly. 'I got a lot to thank yu for.'

Sudden swung into the saddle.

'Same here,' he told the boy. 'Don't yu fret none; I'll be back one o' these days.'

He pulled Nigger's head around and moved easily down the trail, the great black stallion cantering almost silently towards Yavapai. Henry watched the rider until he was swallowed by the darkness, and then, with a sniff, pawed angrily at his eyes.

'Durned night air,' he grumbled. 'Makes a feller's eyes water.'

THE END